BATTLE ROYAL

BATTLE ROYAL

Wallis Peel

CHIVERS

British Library Cataloguing in Publication Data available

This Large Print edition published by BBC Audiobooks Ltd, Bath, 2009.
Published by arrangement with the Author.

U.K. Hardcover ISBN 978 1 408 45660 6
U.K. Softcover ISBN 978 1 408 45661 3

Printed and bound in Great Britain by
CPI Antony Rowe, Chippenham and Eastbourne

Dedication

*To my oldest pal
Ann Orme*

At the time of this story, the middle of the sixth century, there were three distinct cultures in Britain each of which had its own names for the various towns. There were the Celtic-British: the Romano-British and the Saxons.

To simplify matters for readers I have used modern place names throughout with the exception of that where the battle took place. It was called Deorham. Today it is known as Dyrham which modern name derives from the Old British of Dwr for water and Ham for village.

It is situated a little distance north of Bath.

ONE

Ralf muttered beneath his breath, then pulled his horse back to a walk and signalled with one hand. He knew Bracha rode just behind him and he was also aware he had been very aloof since they left. She would be itching to talk and find out what had been decided.

Bracha drew her mount alongside and cast him a thoughtful look, then had to grin. He looked so put out. Father and daughter were unalike physically, because Ralf was dark, and she had a natural, vivid fairness. Old family stories held that Ralf was descended from pure Roman stock that had settled in the area decades ago. He certainly had dark hair and nut-brown eyes, which were not common, whereas Bracha was a replica of her mother Elesa. Her hair was fair and her eyes a light, sky blue.

They were poles apart in temperament. Bracha had not yet learned to control her naturally hot temper, while Ralf was a calm thinker and very self-contained. At thirty-one years, he was heading rapidly into middle age, while his daughter at sixteen years was still entitled to explode more quickly than was prudent; yet he loved her dearly. They often fought for the sheer hell of it. Bracha took after him for brains and she was quick to make

1

a decision so Ralf knew she was often impatient with his more reasoned thought.

Ralf also knew he was not the only one frequently annoyed with her because she could be very stubborn; with a logic that defied him. His wife Elesa had almost washed her hands of their daughter. Her best friend Ygraine would get exasperated. Riwalus, just two years older than Bracha, did not try to understand her. The elders of their tribe were inclined to look down their noses at her, his only surviving child.

It was obvious that Riwalus, despite being a fine fighter and provider, was getting exactly nowhere with his courtship of Bracha so soon his eyes would be bound to wander elsewhere. It was more than high time that Bracha was married. At sixteen years, she was just about on the shelf. Ralf knew he should really look into this matter but first things came first, and his daughter's love life and marriage had to take a backseat.

Bracha had a shrewd idea of the line of her father's thoughts, and she stiffened uneasily. Surely they were not going to have another row? Ygraine said she was too choosy for her own good, which always made Bracha smart. Ygraine was a fine one to talk because, although the same age, she had not promised herself to anyone either.

Bracha's mind switched to Ygraine, and she thought of Ricole, then a wicked grin touched her lips for a second. Ricole was a shade older and did not like Bracha at all, which feeling was reciprocated in full. Between them was natural antipathy and, Bracha suspected, one day there would be the most almighty row and, quite likely, they would fight. Ricole fancied Riwalus who, in turn, had eyes only for Bracha. It was a circumstance in which, if everyone had spoken their minds, they would have cleared the air instead of filling it with heavy scowls.

When Ricole glowered she always reminded Bracha of surly Melwas, one of her bodyguards. He was constantly like a bear just after emerging from a long winter's hibernation. Melwas disliked Bracha, and she heartily wished she could dispense with him but, as a chief's daughter, she had little choice in whom the elders selected as a personal escort. Certainly, there were areas when it was imprudent to push her father too far. The choice of his daughter's bodyguard was one. He would automatically back the elders to the hilt.

Now Gandar, Ygraine's brother, was a splendid fellow He always had a beaming smile, was genuinely affable and a pleasure to be with—sometimes more so than his sister. Ygraine was one of nature's natural gossips, and there were times when she was a burden to have around.

'Stop wool gathering!' Ralf grated at her. 'I

called you for a reason!'

'Yes, Father!' Bracha made herself say meekly.

Ralf threw her a sharp look at this rare compliance, went to say something sour and thought better of it. He looked over at her. She had dressed with a little more elegant care for this visit and looked almost smart for once instead of roaming around dressed like a disreputable slave girl. She wore a leather coat, made from a wolfskin, her well-worn trousers were of the best quality wool, spun in their vill and dyed a dark brown. Her feet were shod in tan-coloured ankle boots, each of which had a sole separate from its upper. This was quality footwear, made by their own slaves. Her cloak was the only splash of colour. It was the bright scarlet of the autumn berries and fastened at the neck with a gold pin shaved in a twist like a deer's antlers. Around her neck she wore a thin torque of gold to note her rank. Attached to her belt, on the left was a short sword that, with its keen edge, was suitable for slashing, as well as stabbing. On the opposite side was a tin bladed dagger. They and her escort, who also carried spears and shields, were perfectly capable of defending these two senior tribal members.

Ralf was aware that Bracha waited for him to speak but his mind had darted off and he sighed without reason.

'How can anyone make arrangements with

an erratic person like him?'

Ralf nodded. She had given an excellent estimation with which he concurred. The great trouble was that none of the three kings could be considered brilliant. He sighed heavily. Rank was all very well, but it could be a burden, and never more so than now. It was the ruling class who had to carry the load of administration, and all the problems that went with this. Freemen paid their nobles a food rent but, in turn, had martial obligations: just as the king received tribute from his chiefs and lesser nobles.

What an easy life his slave had in comparison, Ralf mused. Although virtually of no financial value they were always well fed and clothed by sensible owners because they were property. It paid to look after them well. Just as it did with the other animals. It was only common sense, surely, Ralf asked himself? This meant a slave had no worries so was in a lucky position in life. That a slave would never agree with this reasoning did not occur to him.

'What did you think of King Farinmail?' he asked his daughter suddenly.

Bracha pulled a face. 'He dithers too much for my taste,' she told him shrewdly, 'yet I bet when he does make a decision he is inclined to go off like a mad bull.' The elders might not agree with this neat summing up when they asked Ralf to describe the characters and

5

abilities of their three local kings, yet knew how very vital they were. Especially now.

He gave a wry smile. 'King Coinmail is older than Farinmail and inclined to err on the side of ultra caution all the time while King Condidan is much too arrogant for his own good. I suppose that is to be expected, as he is the King of Cirencester, with the largest following and the best town. So he fancies himself!'

Cirencester was very important, large, well populated and wealthy, far exceeding both Bath and Gloucester. Its king had always looked down his regal nose at all other inhabited areas with their respective kings. None could do this better than Condidan. Was it at all likely that one day Britain would have an overall king or dux, like the ancient Bretwalda? At the moment that was an impossible dream.

'Will you be going to see the other two kings as well?' Bracha asked with interest. Would she be invited to go as well? It was delicious, to get away from the home region.

'I'll certainly have to see them now,' Ralf told her, 'because I can smell trouble coming with a vengeance. What is your history like?'

Bracha stifled a groan. What a time for a verbal examination! But she complied, because she sensed her father was more than a little testy. It would be a total disgrace to have a row in public with the guards flapping their ears.

'When the Romans left, Britain was in trouble. It was owned they gave us excellent roads, first-class administration and coinage, but it all fell to pieces when the legions left our shores to go back to Rome and the trouble there. It was after the departure of the legions when the rot finally set in. We had no coinage, money became scarce, people not working when the factories had to close and civil administration went to ruin. I mean the roads, water and sewerage. It was then that mercenaries came and started to settle here, most of whom had been trouble-making fighters. It was King Vortigen, then the Bretwalda who invited the Jutes, Hengist and Horse, to come to Kent,' and she grinned. 'But as soon as they did come Vortigen had a big row with them and they fought.'

'What was *the* biggest error though?' Ralf persisted. So far so good.

That was easy to answer, and Bracha agreed with what she had been taught. 'Why, inviting the Saxons and Angles in because it gave them big ideas. The Saxons were land hungry, and ours is far superior to the land on the Continent. So once here they would not budge.'

Ralf grunted and nodded. 'It was a foolish thing to do, and now it's going to be us who have to pay the bill,' he said a little sourly, under his breath.

'Artorius fought the Saxons though,' Bracha

reminded him. 'He beat them at Mons Badonis!'

'True!' Ralf agreed. 'And that has given us forty years' breathing space. But now it's all been used up. You heard what I said to Farinmail, and he agreed as well.'

'You think there's going to be war then, Father?'

He nodded. 'Without any doubt. King Ceawlin has been too quiet for far too long, and now that the winter is ending my gut tells me something is going to happen and for once it's high time we were prepared. We must be united this time. Political differences must be tossed aside. Then perhaps we can crush him. If we fight as individuals there will be no chance for us at all. It is imperative that all three local kings agree to merge their forces for a joint defence. Ceawlin will then fail against us.'

King Ceawlin, with his brother Cutha were, in Ralf's opinion, permanent thorns stuck in British flesh. It was nine years ago that the two clever brothers had driven King Ethelbert back into Kent, and a mere three years ago that they had achieved a number of great victories against the Britons, which had extended their Saxon-held territory far beyond the Thames valley.

'That man is coming for us,' Ralf growled.

Bracha blinked. 'But why should he?'

Ralf turned to her. She must be made to

8

understand. 'Because he wants all land to be Saxon as far as the Western seas. That would split the British tribes up and fragment us. Those in the South West will then be cut off from the rest and Ceawlin could pick us off easily one at a time. I did manage to make King Farinmail see this. But what hard work. He is so obtuse! I hope the other two are brighter!'

Ralf gave her a smile. There were Saxon settlers, who often crossed the frontier to set up home on tribal lands but they rarely caused trouble. There were also the Romano-Britons who were descended from Romans who had stayed on in retirement and married British women instead of going back to Rome when their engagements expired. They too did not cause trouble unlike the Saxon warriors.

Although completely untravelled, Bracha had an excellent working knowledge from maps drawn in her geography lessons. She was able to visualise the danger of such fragmentation, and she pulled a face.

'Ceawlin has been quiet these last six years, hasn't he?' she asked with a frown.

'Exactly!' Ralf snapped. 'He has been too quiet for too long, and that state of affairs won't last. You mark my words! We will have to fight and win hands down, because otherwise there will be nothing but trouble in the future.'

Bracha was startled, although she realised

everything said was true. It had not entered her head, prior to this talk, that Ralf considered the situation with such gravity.

To call a council and get all the three kings to agree was just about unheard of: they had managed to unite against a common and local foe, but it had not lasted long before they were back to their usual state of tribal quarrels. Then a new thought struck her.

'Where do the settlers stand? Will they turn against us with a knife in our back, will they go over to the Saxons?' she asked quietly.

Many settlers were in trade and valuable to both sides. Horses, cattle, slaves, hounds were all traded for salt and wines and other goods from the Continent, which had to come through Saxon-held territory. Ralf considered his daughter's question: they would keep well out of a war, more content on trading with both sides and making money, because they were business people.

'Is it possible any new settlers have been planted to spy on us?' Bracha asked suddenly.

'It is possible,' Ralf agreed, 'which is why we never tell them anything. We treat them as neutrals until we discover otherwise and if they are treacherous, we kill them. It's as simple as that. I don't somehow think they will turn against us. They are much too interested in running their businesses and making money. There is also another point. These settlers run their businesses from their homes, and they have their women and children with them. This makes them extra vulnerable. As for the Romanos, I have heard that some of them have left their isolated villas for the safety of the towns, which makes rather a smell to my way of thinking. What do they suspect? I have also heard that some left it a bit too late. Barbarians sailed up the Avon and Severn, landed, went in for their usual rape and butchery and robbed to their hearts' content. The Romanos who had not gone had no chance at all, even those with plenty of slaves. The Barbarians then went back to their ships and sailed off merrily to plunder somewhere else!'

Bracha had not known about this, and it made unpalatable thinking. She saw they were nearly home and Ralf lifted his hand in greeting to one of the perimeter sentries as they walked their tired horses into the large clearing that made home. As she dismounted and gave her horse to the slave Calthus, Bracha heard her name called and closed her eyes for a second in resignation.

'I've being waiting ages for you!' Ygraine cried, running over. 'Tell me all about it!' she bubbled, delighted to have her friend back and dying for a good gossip.

Ygraine was as slender with whippy muscles as Bracha was built upon more solid lines. They had apparently nothing in common, yet between them lay a sound friendship, although

11

Ygraine knew she was often in awe of her friend. Bracha had such a strong character with a temper to match, which made it wise to leave her alone on some occasions.

Ygraine had a delicate bone structure, with long, slender fingers while those of Bracha were short, more perfect for holding a weapon as they were thick and strong. Ygraine was no trained fighter, though she had, like all other females, gone through training. Fighting was not Ygraine's idea of life. What she wanted was to be a healer, and already she had an outstanding knowledge of many plants and herbs. One day, it was her fervent wish that she would be selected by one of the wise older women for detailed instruction. She knew she must have more years before such a post could be offered to her. Until then all she was able to do was look after the animals and the slaves.

It was only the previous autumn that Calthus had been purchased with running sores on one arm. It was Ygraine, who had gone out of her way to cure him. He was a dark-haired, dour man in his thirties, who spent most of his work-time looking after the horses, for which he had considerable talent. Indeed, Ygraine was the first to admit that Calthus had taught her much when he did to decide to speak, because Calthus was, in everyone's opinion, a surly man who had never been worth the price paid when bought from some Romanos.

12

Now Bracha knew Ygraine would expect to hear everything, chapter and verse of where they had been, all she had seen and exactly what had been said by everyone. This was quite out of the question until the elders had been notified. Ygraine's tongue flowed as fast as a river in a spate and also, to make matters worse in Bracha's eyes, Ygraine was incredibly sharp. What she did not know she often guessed, with uncanny accuracy.

Bracha turned to her. 'Don't start to badger me as soon as I get home because you know nothing can be divulged just yet!' she managed to get in first.

Ygraine's face fell with chagrin, and her mind promptly started to rocket in all directions.

'Ygraine! Don't!' Bracha grated.

Her friend threw her a saucy grin. 'Oh very well,' she replied, highly amused. Bracha wore her solemn look so whatever it was, it could not be good. She tipped her head sideways, pursed her lips, all of which made Bracha groan inwardly.

'I'll tell the chief and the elders if you guess anything aloud!' she threatened.

'You wouldn't!' Ygraine gasped.

'No?' Bracha drawled. 'Try me!'

Ygraine lapsed into hurt silence, gave a shrug which did not fool Bracha one bit and sniffed . . . All this silly mystery when soon everyone would know.

'So, you two have condescended to come home, have you?' Elesa said, coming from their home to eye her daughter.

Between mother and daughter was another bone of contention, because Elesa was shocked to have an unmarried daughter of Bracha's age on her hands. There was constant argument between them of Bracha's cavalier treatment of young men, which exasperated Elesa, but she did not push hard like Ralf. He was inclined to overdo matters at times. Elesa had her own memories and a tale known only to one other person and one day, she thought, I'll have to tell Bracha. Yet Riwalus was a handsome young man, so why did Bracha give him such a complete run-around? Who exactly was she looking for? Some dream man not yet born? Always at this point, her maternal exasperation, would make her shake her head, yet between them was affection. Ygraine had no parents, only her beloved brother Gandar, and Elesa wanted to mother her as well, which was why the two girls spent so much time together.

Elesa's eyes warmed as Ralf strode to her, opening his arms wide to give her his usual bear hug. How she loved him, for all his faults including more than a little pomposity. There were many chiefs worse than him, and very few better.

TWO

Calthus stood the animal in the river and let the cold water run over the swollen tendon. He was glad he had been given work with the horses, though most were, in his eyes, nothing but large ponies. They were strong though, and had endurance, vital qualities for long-distance riding. If he had to go into house slavery it would have been the end, he told himself. At least looking after all these animals he had a degree of free movement, and he was extra fortunate in that the chief's household had bought him.

There were just over a dozen slaves in the small community, and Calthus knew he had been lucky if a slave could count such luck as a blessing, when sold like an animal. Now that he had become familiar with the people here, he realised his financial value was certainly not as high as that of a stallion or best breeding mare. With that he supposed he had to be content but he writhed inside. He hated slavery. He had been hauled out, hands restrained and prodded and poked like a beast, then sold to the highest bidder.

To start with, the people had watched him carefully. Each night he was confined in secure quarters and had a sentry over him during the day. With the advent of winter, and his seeming compliance, the guard had been relaxed. More to the point though, was the question to where he could run before the warriors caught him. Such an event would be a horrendous experience, because they would have a legitimate reason to use him for sport and one or two were very cruel. Especially that big pig Melwas.

The chief himself was all right. He had the welfare of his animals and slaves at heart. All were fed, sheltered and clothed to the best of the chief's ability. Elesa, his wife was also kind. He did not care for their daughter. Sometimes, she was a little too cocky as if aware of her high position in life and one day he knew she was going to see her pride come crashing down. That would be interesting.

Ygraine was adorable. If he were younger, in his twenties, and free, he would not mind running a courtship there. She was a kind girl, exceedingly bright and very good with all animals, as well as people. She did not have a dark thread in her character but Ricole did. That girl was spiteful and loathed Bracha yet Calthus knew in a fight Ricole would have no chance at all. He had watched the chief's daughter busy at her weapons' practice and had been astonished at her smooth ability. She equalled most men, and bettered more than a few. He would not care to cross blades with her.

Ygraine's brother Gandar was an ordinary,

happy young man, who was wasting his time trying to catch Bracha's eyes. Why couldn't he see that Ricole was besotted with him? Calthus found all this very strange. Was it because, as a slave, he was an outsider? He could look inwards and see what others failed to note even when under their noses.

Calthus was disinterested in mixing with the other slaves. He found them incredibly insular. Some had been born into slavery, where he was freeborn and only horrible chance had placed him in this invidious position. With this chosen isolation, he took his amusement in observing the many complex relationships around him because he was a shrewd and discreet observer.

He respected the elders. They were five ancients, who held the vills' strings in their adroit hands, and who made the final decisions when the facts were placed before them. He was more than a little in awe of their accumulated wisdom, and often wished he could sit at their feet and listen when they pontificated. That, of course, was out of the question for a slave.

Calthus knew just about everything. He had keen ears and little to distract his mental occupations as he observed, remembered, guessed and played a little game in which he held the fortunes of this place and these people in his hands. They were not fools, far from it, but he found some of their decisions difficult to grasp.

Their temperament was unknown to him. They would row and fight in an instant over a wrong word. So now he understood they were considering unification. The very idea amused him but he kept this attitude hidden behind an artificial, almost bovine, mask.

It was true there were days when he looked back down the months and sighed unhappily. Many a night before he dropped off to sleep, his thoughts whirled unhappily. For how long would he be a slave? If he knew that he could stand it better.

*   *   *

Ceawlin, King of the Saxons, was thoroughly dissatisfied, and he stood outside his home, feet slightly apart, but planted firmly on the grass as if rooted there. He stared broodingly at some nearby trees, very conscious that his small group of nobles, his personal guards, were nearby but, uncertain of his mood, preferring to keep their distance.

Ceawlin tossed his head back and let his short, cropped hair flap in the light breeze. He was the undisputed king from a long line of royal leaders, who went back to his great-grandfather Cerdic, who had died in 534. Cerdic's son Creoda had not lived long enough to reign so this honour had fallen to Cynric, father of Ceawlin.

It was seventeen years ago that Cynric had died and Ceawlin had been automatically elected as Saxon king and overlord. He smiled pensively. He had loved his father and fighting in battle with him had been a wonderful experience. It had also made excellent training for his present position.

Ceawlin allowed his thoughts to roll over the British people. They were an aggressive race, though he did wonder how many of them were aware of the fact they already had Angli blood in their proud veins? It was not all that long ago that many Britons had migrated to the continent. The Germanic race had welcomed them enthusiastically, and the King of the Franks had met them himself with open arms, because there was no doubt that they were a worthy race.

After the Thuringian war, many of these Britons, now called Anglis, had even received noble grants, as well as intermarrying with continentals. So how was it they resented the Saxons? Were they never satisfied?

The Anglis who crossed the sea were fine fighters and made excellent settlers. It was only the need for land expansion that had forced the Saxons to consider settlement themselves on this wet and misty island. So many people moved around on the continent in a vast, mass migratory horde that good land became very precious and scarce.

The South of Britain fascinated the Saxons.

The soil was fertile despite the raw cold climate, but the trouble was, the Britons failed to appreciate these new neighbours. They showed their natural traits of stubbornness, antagonism, belligerence and opinionated views.

Had Cynric's kinsmen, Stuff and Wihtgar, known what they were starting when they sailed to Britain? It was true, they had reached the Island of Wight and expected their lot to have improved. Quite the reverse. The Britons simply would not have it. They wanted the Saxons gone, as for four centuries they had waited for the Romans to depart.

There was only one answer, Ceawlin knew, and that was to crush the Britons once and for all. Which was the best way? When should he make his move? More to the point, how many British warriors would face his men? Where would they make their stand? It was their land, so they would choose, not him. Who would they select as their leader? Would they be able to stop rowing among themselves to select a new Bretwalda? How great were their horse herds? His mind seethed with questions, all of which could yield the information vital for a king to have as he prepared to make war.

Ceawlin sniffed to himself. He had never been backward at coming forward, and this multitude of questions had bothered him for months. Was it possible to thrash the Britons in one battle, man-to-man? This was the greatest enigma of them all. There was little to choose between them and the Saxons, and this was hardly surprising when he considered the Britons' mixed bloodlines.

It was impossible to treat with them because they had an abhorrence of all treaties, which probably went back to the Romans and their habit of conquering by making tribes clients of Rome. The Britons in this southern land were, he knew, held in high contempt by those in the west so it was obvious this year he had to act decisively.

The Britons in the southwest were in a very strong position. They had natural allies in the north, as well as in the southwest tip of the island.

'My plan must be foolproof!' he muttered to himself sagely. He'd already had ideas for over a year and one plan was in operation, but he now desperately needed current facts. So obviously there was only one thing to do. The next step was preordained.

He turned on his heel and strode a few more paces, thinking hard. He dressed as a king should. He wore finely woven blue trousers, which ended in thin neat crossed garters which were a deeper blue than his trousers. His tunic was of the best wool, a light tan shade, which complemented the rest of his dress. This was fastened at one corner with a very elaborate gold brooch made in the shape of a bear's paw. His shoes were highly sophisticated and cut from one piece of fine, light brown leather, fastened with a strap and toggle.

He wore his hair very short and neat, and it framed his face, which was a little thickset and marred on one cheek with a long scar. His eyes were a very pale blue, which, in a certain light, appeared to be grey. Perhaps his lips were a little too thin; certainly, when angry, they seemed to vanish into his square jaw.

On one hip he wore his jewelled scramasax (a Saxon dagger) and on the other his craftsman-made sword. This was very famous, as it had been pattern-welded to make it extra strong and whippy. It was a fearsome weapon, with the hilt decorated with twinkling jewels and kept in a scabbard lined with sheep's fleece, so that natural grease would halt rust. This sword hung from his left hip supported by a baldric from a shoulder.

His small clothes were also light blue, made from the best linen. He was very clean and smelled of herbs because, like all of his race, he took great personal care concerning dress and cleanliness.

He appeared to stroll about aimlessly but Ceawlin could feel the eyes of his gesith upon him and he smothered a grin. There were times when these nobles fussed more than a mother hen. From an eye corner he spotted another watcher, and his grin was swept away with a scowl. Who else could manage that?

It was Cenberht his bastard son and, that reminded him, he would soon have to do something about the betrothal as well. Eadgifu was fifteen years old, just a little younger than his handsome son and already he had approached her father Ceolwulf about a possible match. Only just in time as well, as there had been another noble sniffing around.

He was a widower, and did have a legitimate son, so Cenberht was placed in a peculiar position. Not that he seemed to care, Ceawlin thought sourly. It was true, he kept out of the king's way unless summonsed and his teachers spoke highly of his mental abilities. It was his weapons' talents that were lacking. Cenberht could use all of the normal weapons, but he never seemed to put in any effort. It was as if they were all a huge joke—which was heresy to any well-bred Saxon.

He was so confoundedly good-looking too. He took after his long dead mother whom Ceawlin had meant to marry once he learned she was pregnant. He had instead gone off with his father to fight battles and when he returned the girl was dead, and the bawling baby was left alone.

Cenberht was very tall, with long, lean muscles, which gave enormous strength and endurance, often beating the more bulging variety like those possessed by the king and his brother Cutha. He was like a deer in flight when he ran lightly on his toes, as graceful as any maiden and the whole was topped by a face of classical Greek beauty. He was so lovely to look at, that, a while ago, Ceawlin had been forced to ask about this son as doubts had arisen concerning his masculinity. He had been adequately reassured by Cenberht's tutors in the most positive way when he made a slave girl pregnant.

Although a bastard, Cenberht was a thegn, with a high wergild and he, as king, intended to improve upon this when the time was opportune. He would end up a highly valued earldorman and adviser in Council, a position great with respect and dignity.

Ceawlin swung towards his gesith. 'Where is Cutha?' he shouted, suddenly very impatient.

'Over there, sire!' one member replied, nodding sideways.

Ceawlin stood and shook his head. Cutha could exasperate him as much as Cenberht. He had been given an offering from a woman's cooking pot, and now, aimlessly taking all the time in the world, he strolled back, gnawing at a luscious titbit.

'You will end up with a knife in your guts,' Ceawlin snapped at him. 'She is married, you know!'

Cutha was unimpressed. 'Her old man's away so I can't let her cook for nothing, now can I?' he replied reasonably, but he grinned from ear to ear as he finished chewing.

Ceawlin felt like stamping with anger.

Cutha considered life a big joke, and did not have one serious hair on his head. 'Why can't you act more Royal?' Ceawlin grated.

Cutha chuckled. 'You do it better for both of us, brother!' he replied, but not unkindly. Not for all the land in this island would Cutha willingly become king. If anything happened to Ceawlin, then his legitimate son could have the position and welcome to it. If still too young, as at present, then a Regent would have to be arranged; just as long as Cutha did not have to be serious.

'Oh come on inside and try to act your age!' Ceawlin grumbled and waved to his gesith, all of whom followed with alacrity.

Cuthwulf, always known by his diminutive, was unabashed as he finished off the last of the meat on the bone and tossed it with an accurate aim to an expectant hound.

'I want Cenberht in here as well,' Ceawlin shouted, feeling his temper rise. Was he mad having both of them in here when trying to plot serious tactics, because they both tried his patience to the limit? Still, he told himself, he would wipe the grin off one face and liven up the other before the day was ended.

Easa and Crida sat down with Octa, and some of the others. They waited expectantly, though they threw each other puzzled looks. The king had obviously thought of something, but what?

Octa was a little older than the others in his

middle thirties, and sometimes, Cutha told himself, he acted as if he had one foot in the grave. He should loosen up and get with it. Easa and Crida were opposites, yet good friends and foils to each other. Crida was serious, while Easa could tell a rip-roaring story, usually verging on the obscene yet still humorous. It was Cenberht who stood out like the sore thumb when he joined in. His incredible handsomeness, unmarred by battle scars, his tall bearing with natural dignity and refinement, plus his quiet ways, made him unusual enough to be viewed askance. If he had not been the king's son, albeit illegitimate, he would have had a hard life being constantly baited.

Ceawlin's home was the largest in the permanent compound, as was only fitting for a king. The hall of his house had a side room in which he conducted his meetings. When on the march of course he used a tent like anyone else.

The home was graciously furnished to a high standard, with many animal pelts, all finely tanned, which were scattered generously around and some of which were hung from the wooden walls as decoration. Spare weapons were fixed at the walls in distinctive patterns yet were easy to grab in an emergency.

There were trestle tables on three sides of the large room, and on the fourth were sleeping cubicles. The cooking fires were at the top of the great room, and these walls were black from soot.

The servants were of both sexes and all slaves, some of whom had served the king for years. Guards proliferated, each armed to the teeth. A few women flitted in and out, though the female sex was in the minority in this tun, which had been constructed rather hastily with war in mind.

Ceawlin's personal slave was waiting beside his master as he sat on his elaborately carved, high stool, then he poured fresh ale from a new batch. Other slaves served the remaining men and Cutha delighted in its fresh, biting tang. Just what was needed after hot meat.

Ceawlin nodded, and the slaves disappeared, though he knew some would position themselves to eavesdrop. Keeping a secret here was difficult.

'Right!' he stated firmly. 'This year it will be war against the Britons!' Ceawlin eyed his men, and was pleased to note a glow enter their eyes. 'Something tells me the time is right!'

'Outright war, no truces or treaties?' Cutha asked for all of them. It made a huge difference.

Ceawlin nodded. At long last Cutha showed a bit of sense and some interest. His brother could, at times, be remarkably astute when he decided to halt treating life as a jest.

Ceawlin shook his head. 'No, the usual. All

those taken prisoner, and who swear allegiance to me, will live as free men and women. Those who don't—slavery!' he stated bluntly. 'It is pointless, setting out to butcher every man, woman and child. The news would race through this island like wildfire, and it would only give us more problems in the long run. We do it this way, and perhaps some of the other knuckleheaded Britons will get the message and come down on our side, without more fighting.'

'Where, sire?' Octa asked.

Ceawlin gave him a thoughtful look. 'You know perfectly well. There is only one place to go this year, west then north.'

It was as Octa had thought. 'There are settlers in that area, and some are Saxons. Will the Britons take their spite out on our people?'

It was a good point. 'I don't know,' Ceawlin admitted honestly, 'but when settlers cross the frontier to strike out on their own they have to take the rough with the smooth, don't they?'

'What about Romanos?' Easa wanted to know.

Ceawlin shook his head. 'The Britons don't bother them. I think they regard them all as decadent, and I'm inclined to agree with their summing-up. When I think what the Romans were and what the Romanos are—!' He gave a snort of disparagement. 'I don't count them in my plans. I consider them useless, merely decorative.'

Crida spoke next. 'Do you have a positive plan?' he asked, in his deep male voice.

Ceawlin nodded. He had been awaiting this question and knew it would come from Crida, who only dealt in facts, never speculation. 'I do!' Ceawlin confirmed and lowered his voice confidentially. 'Our main problem has always been lack of positive information but I took steps about that quite a while ago. I do know that the River Severn is huge, and my plan is to drive the Britons before me, if it becomes necessary. I calculate such a move would sever their links with the north and the south-west, which means we can pick up the remainder to suit ourselves. It also gives us the use of the river and coastline in due course.'

It was a good plan because it was simple. Cenberht realised its potency immediately, but, as always, said nothing. He just listened. He suspected he was wanted for something in particular; as to what this might be he had no idea. If it meant a journey away he was all for that. His tutor could teach him nothing more, so a chance to stretch his legs and get away from all these people would suit him perfectly.

Crida had been turning something over in his mind. 'We would have to make sure of a very decisive victory after that debacle at Mons Badonicus,' he pointed out. 'We can't afford any more warriors facing us like their Artorius!'

Ceawlin had worked that out months ago. 'They don't have an Artorius now.'

'But they might have a natural leader about whom we know nothing!' Octa observed shrewdly.

Cutha was doubtful. 'What? Britons unite to fight? I'll believe that when I see it happen. They are only really happy rowing among themselves.'

Ceawlin grinned with a wolfish leer. 'That's where we can divide and rule!' And he turned to Cenberht. 'I have a very special task for you because I've been told you speak their tongue fluently. I want you to ride out right through their land—if they will let you—and find out exactly what is going on, where and when. It will be dangerous. Do you have the balls for it?'

Cenberht went scarlet, drew himself up even taller, and to everyone's astonishment appeared to change into another person. His jaw jutted, his eyes glowed hotly, as he snarled, 'They are as good as yours—Father!' he growled.

Ceawlin was as shocked as the rest of them. This was a sudden, new and unexpected side to one he had always considered a dreamer. This son now radiated new and totally unexpected authority. His voice had deepened, and his words rasped. What was more, there was challenge in them.

Cenberht had never dreamed of such a task,

and his heart swelled with glee but he kept his face a harsh mask of just-controlled anger, directed solely at the king. In the past there had been days when the king did not appear to know he even existed. Now he could be out of the tun and totally free to act as he thought fit, which was most satisfying.

Ceawlin nodded approval. So, he told himself, this cub can bite and fight as well. That was a most pleasurable discovery. 'You will have an escort of one, of course,' and he looked over at Crida. 'You! No one goes alone into enemy territory,' he added flatly.

Crida had never really cared for Cenberht until five minutes ago, when the young man had shown his fangs and made clear they were not just for display. 'I doubt the Britons will take kindly to a spy in their midst for even a weekend so our disguise must be very good.'

The king looked at his son. 'Any bright ideas?'

Cenberht nodded. 'I will go as a clerk, a person who is always useful to those who cannot read and write, and who is always accepted. I can manage their Runic writing as well. I could also say I am riding around considering land for possible future settlement. That will be reasonable and logical,' he pointed out. He was not too thrilled at having Crida with him, a man whom he considered old-fashioned, staid, unenterprising and not particularly loaded with brains, but a solitary traveller would be in a very dangerous position.

'How long is all this going to take if you are going to make this look like some oddball mission? Time might be of the essence,' Octa pointed out.

'He's right, brother!' Cutha agreed. He had always liked Cenberht, and if anyone could fill that part to perfection, it was him. All they would need would be two good horses, first-class but normal weapons, plus all the accoutrements any respectable clerk would carry.

Ceawlin then turned his attention to his brother. 'I have work for you as well. I want every fighter exercised and trained for when Cenberht returns, because then we will march. All that running round should remove some of your fat as well!' he mocked.

Cutha had the grace to blush. His waistline had expanded a little. 'Easa can see to supplies with Octa's help.' Cutha turned to the others. 'Your men can assist wherever you might be needed,' and he turned back to the king. 'You go through Bath first?'

Ceawlin shook his head. 'We will travel west, then cut north and avoid Bath. We can always sack that place afterwards.'

Cutha had been thinking on his feet. 'We could do with a code in case something untoward happened and Crida had to come back alone with a message!' he pointed out sagely.

Ceawlin was pleased. When Cutha did stop acting the fool, as well as thinking less of his stomach, he had a good mind, with bright ideas.

Cenberht was ahead of him though. 'There are eight of us present here now, so if I send a written message just read it, with every word starting with the eighth letter along.'

They all stared at him with admiration. He had thought it out so quickly and efficiently and even the king was impressed.

'Well get busy, all of you!' Ceawlin growled, and the gathering broke up. He beckoned Cenberht to follow him outside, where no one could eavesdrop.

'Listen to what I say very carefully and make sure you keep this to yourself—for obvious reasons!' and he spoke rapidly with force.

Cenberht was astonished but also filled with admiration. He swelled with pride as the king continued to confide in him alone.

Ceawlin then changed the subject. 'I also wanted to talk to you, privately about a possible betrothal. I have spoken to a girl's father, of one who would be most suitable for you. I was only just in time as another parent was sniffing around. When you return, you can meet the girl and we will take matters further.'

Cenberht was not sure that he liked any of this. Marriage did not fall within his current plans, and he knew he would be most reluctant to go along with whatever his father had in mind. He decided to say nothing at the present time. The king was in a good mood, pleased with him; it would be very imprudent to cross him just now. His mind still buzzed with the previously imparted information, which had staggered him. He knew his father was a very skilful tactician and strategist, but that which had been confided in him showed he was as cunning as half a dozen foxes.

Ceawlin gave him one more last piece of advice. 'Crida is a good man but tell him only what you think it is necessary for him to know. This is for your own safety. Even the strongest man can be made to talk under torture. Try and get back within the month if at all possible, because time is indeed of the essence!'

THREE

'Now, just you take notice of what I say!' Ralf commanded firmly as they stood near the riding herd. The only other person around was a slave, Calthus, and he didn't count, because he was just a two-legged animal. 'You're not to ride alone anymore. Take Melwas with you!'

Bracha pulled a face. 'I don't like him. He is a nasty man!'

Ralf snorted. 'Nasty or not, he makes a first-class bodyguard, especially now we know there are Saxons around somewhere, and you'll do what you are told for once, without arguing. Do I made myself clear?' he rasped turning into a domineering chief. This was no game they were playing. She must be serious. 'And while I'm at it,' he continued very sternly, 'just watch yourself here!'

Bracha was puzzled. 'I don't understand you?'

Ralf took a deep breath. 'You know that finally all the three kings have agreed for unification in the war, which is coming. It has taken a lot of arranging, quite a lot of dubious politics and considerable fast-talking but there is still much to do. We have selected the site of Deorham, to make our stand for battle, but there are many little matters, like basic logistics, to consider. How many fighters can we muster between us? How many sound horses? How long will it take the men from the Cirencester area to get to Deorham? What about food and water for a great crowd? When we fight on foot where is the best place for the horses to be kept? That is why I am now going to see King Farinmail to iron out these last problems. While I'm away you have to take my place, and the elders will be watching you very carefully. To see how you handle yourself, and the people in general!' he warned.

Ralf paused and was gratified to see his daughter's deep interest. Did he have a personal flutter of doubt about her ability? If so, it was no bad thing. Over-confidence was always more deadly. 'If anything serious happens to us, the fighters will obey you, providing the elders agree. It's *them* you have to impress: Alun, Ulfin and Cador are very good men and don't you forget it either.' He paused and decided to give it her straight. 'You are not at all a popular girl!'

Bracha was startled at this bluntness, then blushed with embarrassment. She already knew this. It rankled and she tipped her head to one side thoughtfully. 'Why not?' she asked honestly.

'Because you can be too acerbic at times,' Ralf replied with equal frankness. 'There is more than one way to go about anything. Try and find a little tact for once. It can work wonders. On the other hand though, be firm when necessary, without being sarcastic or bullying. The people despise weakness, just as bossiness arouses their antagonism. Strike for the middle line at all times and you will find it pays dividends.'

Bracha gulped uneasily. So many instructions! She was not sure that she liked being a chief's daughter after all. How free and easy was Ygraine's life in comparison. Even the despised Ricole could just about do and say as she pleased, whereas now she, Bracha, would have to think long and hard before she did anything. Was it worth it?

Ralf read her easily and chuckled . . . 'Do you good!' he told her quite unsympathetically, then he lifted one hand, and beckoned. 'Slave! I'll ride that stallion when I leave!' he bellowed.

Calthus nodded obsequiously and stifled a grin. 'Will you, master?' he asked himself. 'You might just end up having a rough ride!' It was spring and the mares were coming into season. The stallion might have other ideas, but he reminded himself that he was only a slave. It was not his place to advise a high and mighty. He knew perfectly well he was being downright awkward, and it tickled his fancy, as well as managing to brighten his day fractionally. He had overheard all that had been said. Did these high-ranking people consider slaves deaf, dumb and daft? Or was it because they were considered only another form of animal?

Elesa watched as Ralf rode away, then noted Bracha wandering around apparently aimlessly, then saw she was noting and observing carefully. In her father's absence, Elesa could only hope that Bracha would learn to bottle her temper. It would help if Ricole could manage to refrain from her usual snide remarks—jealous because of Bracha's status and frustrated through her longing for Riwalus. What was wrong with the young people today? Why must they always yearn for the impossible?

She smiled softly at secret thoughts and

Bracha halted in mid-stride, saw this, wondered and walked over. 'Mother, what are you hiding?' she asked, with amusement.

'Oh! Thinking of the past!' Elesa replied dreamily. Deep down, she did not mind Bracha's attitude towards being courted. The girl would marry one day, and it stirred her to wonder what kind of a young man she would pick. Certainly, the local youths appeared to hold no appeal yet there were some fine specimens. Was Bracha being extra fussy or was it a natural instinct?

Bracha was very conscious she was under the critical eyes of the elders whom she now knew were not enthusiastic about her. It was very sobering knowledge. Taking a deep breath, she approached Gandar, whom she liked very much.

'Will you check the scouts are out, and rotate the guards for me, please?' she asked in a polite voice.

Gandar blinked, then nodded with a little smile. What was this? Bracha displaying tact? Wonders will never cease. 'Would you like me to check the slaves' work for you as well?' he prompted.

Bracha bit her lip. 'Oh yes, please!' Then she looked at him. 'What else am I expected to do?'

Gandar grinned. 'Go and make some obsequies to the elders when next you pass!' he advised with a chuckle. 'They can stand on their dignity, especially Alun!'

'Oh goodness yes!' Bracha muttered. She had forgotten them completely. Alun was the senior, very ancient member of their tun, who had reached the quite remarkable age of sixty years. He had a tetchy temper to go with those years. She walked over to where the elders sat close together on their stools outside their homes on the very edge of the clearing. She ducked her head politely and reported what she had done, said and planned.

Alun was dour. He did not like this girl. She was trouble, big trouble and, in his opinion totally unfit ever to become a chief when anything happened to her father. He threw her a brief nod, but decided to be charitable and reserve judgment. The others would follow his lead; they always did, which fact tickled his pride. There had to be something in life to make up for the misery of those joint aches, which came to the old.

Bracha walked away, glad that was over with. Now to check the sentries were alert. It was improbable Saxons would come this way just yet. She saw with a grimace that Melwas stood at one post. Their eye contact was brief. Each heartily disliked the other yet now he was under her command. For a fleeting second it flashed through her mind she could be awkward and give him some outlandish order, but good sense stayed her hand. No matter what she thought of him, Melwas was a brave warrior and a superb fighter.

She strolled a few paces down a path and stood where it angled sharply. This was deliberate: to stop mounted warriors riding full tilt into the tun's area without warning. All their paths were so designed and she considered that they made a good first line of defence.

'Wake up, girl!' a voice said from a bush and Bracha nearly took off with shock. 'I could have been a Saxon and speared you quite easily!'

'Mona!' she gasped, feeling her heart thunder. How on earth did she always manage to creep up on them? She ducked her head low with politeness and prepared to offer an arm because Mona was old. How old, no one knew nor dared to ask because Mona, like all of her kind, was a law unto herself. Even Alun stood respectfully when Mona first appeared and certainly none could beat her in an argument.

Mona moved on to the path. It tickled her fancy to creep up on them and each time she successfully did this it was to the sentries' irritation. She was very old, and her face was a mass of crinkles. Her hair, thin in parts, was heavily frosted. She was not tall and appeared small because of bowed shoulders yet, when she chose, she could step out as briskly as the best of them. Why, Bracha wondered for the umpteenth time, did Mona not get the joint ills like other old people? Was it all part and parcel of her magic? Because Mona knew secrets only shared with those of a like calling.

She was a healer, a soothsayer and a religious of the old Druids' rites. She wandered the land, welcomed wherever she went, was given the best food, and, in return, offered wise advice and healing skills. She answered to no man.

Bracha knew that Ygraine worshipped her and that her dearest wish was to serve as Mona's acolyte when next she elected to take one. Mona was choosy though. Her pupils were expected to have certain qualities combined with a high intellect. They must be devoted to the wildlife and give absolute obedience. Ygraine fitted this bill and Bracha wondered if Mona was only awaiting her friend's advancement in years.

'Will you stay with us, Mona?' she asked delicately.

The old lady eyed her thoughtfully. 'I'll think about it,' she prevaricated.

Mona was in two minds about the chief's daughter. On her last visit Bracha had been brash, outrageously bossy, impatient and thoroughly dislikeable yet she was quiet enough now. Was it possible that the girl had acquired a little more maturity and sense? It made an interesting question and Mona pursed her lips thoughtfully.

Mona knew all. How she understood the

future was something she did not know herself; she simply accepted. It was a gift handed down from her equally farsighted mother and, centuries to come, would cause others like her to be burned at the stake.

Mona knew that her appearance was capable of causing great alarm under specific circumstances, simply because of her prophetic abilities. Like so many of her kind, and all the Druids who had predeceased her, she would usually only answer set question in mysterious riddles, leaving their interpretation to others. She now knew she had to be in this region, and she had walked long and far. She could move with amazing nimbleness, snaring her own meat when far from habitation.

She had no fear of the wild animals. Wolves avoided her with their own psychic senses, both alpha male and female, carefully leading the pack from her path. A she bear with a cub would stop, look with short-sighted piggy eyes, scent, then, as Mona stood silent and unmoving, amble away in another direction. All of the deer would hold their ground and regard her, ears pricked, scenting deeply, but unalarmed. They knew instinctively, this old woman was friend and not foe. Her vibes told them this.

Even the wild cats would back off and retreat to their lairs without a spit or a hiss at her passing. Only the tiny game feared her, although she did not eat a lot of meat. She preferred fish with a copious supply of plant foods, at which she was an expert in selecting for diet, medicine and general good health.

Mona bristled with incredible well-being, putting all other old people to shame. Sometimes she advised people like Alun on what herbs to eat to avoid the joint ills and fevers. She told him how to protect himself in the wet months, but the old man had gone too far down that road for her advice to be practical.

'Take me to your mother!' she snapped suddenly at Bracha who hastened to obey, though her mind whirled. Was it her imagination or did Mona only ever appear when she knew her skill and wisdom would be needed? Was this wonderful or ominous? Bracha had no idea, and knew better than to question the old woman. She wished her father was here.

Elesa met Mona with outstretched hands. Between them was a rare friendship and Elesa was one of the very few people with whom Mona knew she could relax completely. They studied each other. Elesa had worry lines, Mona noted, and she nodded sagely. Her presence was certainly required in this part of the island. Her instincts had, as usual, been accurate.

'I have come to visit,' she said in a soft voice.

Elesa hugged her. 'It's been a long time!'

she replied gently, but also felt alarm. Why here and now? What did Mona sense or know, which was hidden from her? 'Will you lodge with us?'

Mona considered, then shook her head. 'If I remember correctly, you have a small guesthouse, which stands near the stockade fence. I will live there, but take my food with you. I like your broth, and I have some extra herbs for you to put in.'

Bracha realised she was not wanted and stood only a few moments, fidgeting from one foot to the other as Gandar returned to confirm he was satisfied with the slaves' work and the sentries' rotation, then Ygraine trotted into view.

'I'm going out for some fresh plants. Coming?'

'Yes, I will!' Bracha said with some relief. It would be good to get away from all this for a few hours, and she looked at Gandar, eyebrows raised in a silent question. She hoped he would offer to escort them, rather than that bully Melwas. She knew they dared not ride alone. She also knew Ygraine felt a little out of things. All of the slaves were healthy, and Calthus was wholly better. None of the animals were sick and Ygraine had nothing to do. She was bored.

Gandar nodded, grinned understanding and went to fetch their horses. They were soon mounted and with a heavily armed Gandar in their lead they trotted out into the wild. They both eyed land with which they had been familiar since children, but Bracha's knowledge was more in-depth.

She had ridden extensively with her father especially during all the recent meetings with the three kings. She had even ridden as far as Deorham with Ralf as he wished to study the area in detail. He had then about-turned and gone all the long way back on the road nearly to Bath. He had not missed one turning of the many trails on top of the plateau road which ran for so far.

She had been puzzled as to why Deorham had been picked as their battle site by the three kings, especially as the hilltop held no water. It was true that the tiny vill below did have plenty as well as fodder for many horses but she was no military tactician. Her father had seen her bewilderment and tried to explain a little.

'We want a frontal attack,' he had told her and waved one hand from right to left. 'See! The land is open before us. Nothing can be hidden. No nasty surprises. All we have to do is build some good frontal defences, trenches and a rampart. This area also is within decent riding distance for all three of the kings' men. It makes a perfect battlefield.'

Bracha had nodded thoughtfully, and studied everywhere carefully. There were two other hills, not of any great height, only just slightly taller than the one on which they sat their mounts. From these hills anyone would have a bird's eye view of the whole proceedings. She stored this titbit away for possible future reference.

Naturally, she would be expected to fight like all the other female soldiers but they would possibly be held in reserve, which was always a sound policy. Let the enemy throw himself upon the men's weapons then, when he was weakened, call up the female reserves. She wondered, which king would lead or would it be a trio of kings? Condidan would consider himself superior, but it was hardly likely Farinmail and Coinmail would allow him to walk over them. It was true that Condidan, as king of the largest inhabited area, with the greatest number of followers would expect prime position. She did not envy her father, the other chiefs and the respected elders trying to sort out matters that concerned personal pride.

'Say when you want to stop, Ygraine!' she called out to her friend, who nodded.

Ygraine was busily looking around and wool-gathering at the same time. Mona was here! Dare she hope she could talk to her? She bubbled with excitement and longed to discuss this with Bracha and resolved to do so on their return. After all, Bracha was standing in for Chief Ralf, so one of her duties would be to advise.

They had left the heavily wooded region and rode their horses at a slow walk over grassed land with just a few trees and bushes. To one side Ygraine spotted a little copse, and she saw the plants around were of the variety that liked moisture. This meant there had to be a spring somewhere near.

'Over there!' Ygraine cried, and vaulted from her saddle as Bracha copied. Gandar dismounted, more leisurely, after taking a careful look around. He saw nothing untoward in this spot. No one could creep up on them, so he carefully took all three sets of reins and knotted them in a slipknot.

He hefted his spear and watched the girls with amusement. How different they were yet how likeable. Past acid comments about Bracha did not bother him. Deep down, he suspected she had the same fine inner core of her father but this had to develop. Some people could be so impatient and forget that they too had once been very young.

Bracha strolled around, eyes down. What she was seeking were plants and early flowers. She loved colour, even though her trousers and tunics were always brown or dark green, but flowers were another matter. Particularly in the spring, when they pushed up in vivid whites, blues and yellows.

She looked over at Ygraine who was bent double, eyes not missing a single plant or leaf. Ygraine too liked colour, and she wore them.

Today, her trousers were bright yellow with an orange tunic and Bracha thought this made a horrible colour combination. She certainly stood out though, at a distance.

Ygraine slowly ambled forward, sometimes touched a leaf, then discarded the plant. She moved between two shrubs and headed for the tiny copse. Gandar took a deep breath. This air was so fresh and exhilarating and the spring sun's rays were welcome on his face after the winter months, which had been bitter.

He and Bracha were completely relaxed. It was so still, out here. Almost as if they were the only people alive in the world.

Ygraine's scream knifed through the air and made them both jump with shock. It was deep-throated and went on and on, then her voice silenced as if cut off with a knife.

Bracha stood frozen for three heartbeats from sheer shock. Even Gandar's feet were rooted while he collected scattered wits.

'A sow with her sunder!' Bracha cried and snatched out her sword. All the wild boar were highly dangerous at any time, let alone when they had young.

Gandar sprang into action. He charged forward, spear levelled, a snarl on his face. He loved his sister dearly, and her shriek could only have come from downright shock or fear and Ygraine did not frighten easily.

'You go to the right!' Gandar bellowed at Bracha. 'I'll take the left, so we can attack it

48

together but don't make a mistake with boar!'

Bracha had no intention of doing that. She had once seen a good hunter ripped to death by a boar's savagery.

They shot into the trees and saw Ygraine, leaning against a tall tree's trunk, one hand to her mouth, eyes wide open with shock and looking downwards. There was no sign of any wild animal, let alone a boar.

'What is it?' Bracha gasped, looked around and missed where Ygraine pointed because of another tree.

'Down there!' Ygraine shouted. 'He gave me such a shock! I thought I was all alone!'

Gandar elbowed his way past the girls, looked down and instantly lifted his spear to kill.

Bracha acted fast. 'No!' she shrieked. 'It's only a boy!'

Gandar froze, lips drawn back in a snarl, then very slowly he lowered his weapon fractionally and glared downwards.

The boy lay helpless and looked up, wide-eyed from terror, aware that his life swayed in a most precarious balance. He lifted up one hand, in supplication and Ygraine caught her breath. It was the skinniest arm she had ever seen, filthy dirty, bleeding from thorns and brambles and her heart flip flopped over.

'Don't, brother!' she screeched. 'I found him. He is mine, all mine!'

FOUR

Cenberht was fed up. This was not turning out as he had thought, because Crida was so dour. He only spoke when necessary but Cenberht did not mind this. An idle chatterer would have irritated him. What stuck in his throat was the fact that his escort took his orders very seriously. He had been told to guard the king's son, which meant Cenberht could not relax anywhere until Crida had assessed their situation.

Cenberht knew something was brewing. He rarely lost his temper but when he did he always astonished those around. It never entered his head that Crida was not so enthusiastic about this journey, because Crida did not particularly like Cenberht and had always considered him a liability upon the Saxon race as a whole. That he might have hidden depths was only now dawning upon him and he was uncertain how to handle this new situation.

'What's eating you?' Cenberht said, pulling up his mount and eyeing Crida coldly.

Crida also stopped and returned the look with a stolid expression. 'I don't know what you mean!' he grunted.

Cenberht sniffed. 'You are a lousy liar. I know what it is. You didn't really want to come, because it's me, isn't that so?' he challenged.

Crida thought, *'If that's how you want it, you can have it!'* 'Yes!'

For a few seconds Cenberht was taken aback. 'Why?' he snapped. It was better to have this out, here and now, before they went another step forward.

Now, it was Crida's turn to analyse himself. Why did he have this dislike for the king's son? Cenberht had never done anything to him. Indeed, he had always been civil or appeared distant. That was no crime. Others had far worse attributes. He plunged wildly and did not give a damn. With luck, they could have a flaming row and return home for someone else to do this job. 'You don't act like a king's son!'

Now it was Cenberht's turn to be momentarily lost for words. 'I don't know what you mean! I can't help being a bastard!'

Crida pulled a rough face, which could have meant anything. 'You are too airy-fairy, head in the clouds, too fond of mooning over plants, writing and animals instead of acting like a warrior. Some of the girls put on a better show than you!'

'You can have them then,' Cenberht retorted angrily. 'Who wants a masculine female? I don't!'

They glowered at each other, contempt blatant but now at an impasse. Cenberht got in first. 'So what do you want to do about it?

51

Fight? You might just have to eat your words!'
He barked his challenge.

This was nearly too much for Crida, but he
managed to retain his temper with a struggle.
'Brave words!' he jeered. 'We fight and I kill
you so what do you think the king would do to
me? Oh! You are very safe to issue a
challenge!'

Cenberht went scarlet as Crida's truth
struck home. For a few seconds he had no
retort, which would suffice. 'This is not going
to work out,' he said finally. 'You'd better get
yourself back safely, I'll go on alone!!'

That alarmed Crida . . . 'Oh no you won't!
And I'd be in an even worse position, and you
know it, king's son!' he snapped.

Cenberht knew a few more words, and they
would be fighting. His honour had been
impugned, his integrity questioned, but some
of Crida's words had gone home. He took a
deep breath. 'Shall we start afresh?' he
offered. 'And get on with the matter at hand?'
He wondered what Crida would say if he knew
about the private conversation the king had
held with him. It was totally impossible for him
to turn back because of this confidence. Too
much was at stake.

Crida too had been reviewing his situation
and, gloomily, he realised he was stuck with it.
Then a streak of honesty surfaced. Perhaps the
king saw something that had escaped his eyes.
He nodded slowly and offered a limp grin.

'Then let's ride on!' Cenberht told him. If they did run into trouble, how reliable would this man be? It was an unpleasant question in his mind.

With a grunt that could have meant anything, Crida nodded, and both pushed their horses into a slow canter.

'We must be careful. We could be near habitation!' Cenberht warned.

Crida braked instantly. 'Whose?'

'Settlers—I hope—not Britons just yet,' Cenberht told him, remembering the information given by the king. 'Anything could be over that slope!' he warned.

Just before the top they dismounted, tied their horses together, then slid forward on their bellies through the long grass to spy downwards. They studied the clearing below on three sides of which were trees while the fourth held the bottom of their slope.

'Two homes,' Crida murmured, 'and big ones as well. That means they must have plenty of slaves as guards.'

'I think they are our people,' Cenberht told him. 'The king has not heard of any Romanos around here but he has heard of a strong Saxon settlement. This has to be it!'

'Let's go down and see what happens!' Crida suggested.

Cenberht grinned, their recent animosity forgotten now there was the chance of some action. They checked the looseness of their weapons, mounted their horses, crested the top of the slope and walked their horses gently down towards solid fencing and sudden human activity.

The settlers showed they were highly alert. They were spotted immediately and many armed slaves appeared through the gate.

'They have had trouble, or are expecting it,' Cenberht remarked.

'They certainly moved quickly. And look at their arms! Those two men at the front must be the owners!' Crida agreed.

To show peaceable intent, they stopped their horses a number of paces before what had now become a large gathering of men who bristled with weapons. Cenberht noted that the land in one direction was tilled. Behind the two large buildings was a very large herd of horses on one side and cattle on the other. About the whole establishment was an air of solidity and considerable affluence. The whole place was almost a fortification.

'Greetings to you!' Cenberht called out as they stopped and awaited an invitation to dismount.

'Who are you and what do you want?' one of the better-dressed men called out in the Saxon tongue. At the same time, the well-trained slaves had moved forward and discreetly surrounded them. Both Cenberht and Crida ignored this circling movement and kept their eyes rigidly on this obvious master of the establishment.

'I am Cenberht, a travelling clerk, and this is my man Crida who escorts me,' he told them smoothly.

'From where?' the other challenged suspiciously. Anyone could dress in another's clothes for disguise and come riding up as a decoy only to be followed by warriors when the gates were wide open.

'Back there!' Cenberht replied and waved a hand firmly in the direction from which they had come. He appreciated that all settlers who wilfully crossed the frontier into enemy territory had to be unpredictable. They were more likely to hit first and ask questions later.

A second, better-dressed man approached with wary eyes. He held a sword at the ready. 'What is the name of the brother to the king?' he demanded to know.

'Cutha, of course!' Cenberht told him. 'And he is getting fat around his middle!'

'Where will the king's son fight in his army?' was the next probing question.

Cenberht gave a sigh. 'I would be astonished if he fought anywhere, at his tender years when he is still working with his tutors. We are not Britons in disguise. There is no horde of warriors waiting back there. We are just two rather tired travellers and will be grateful for hot food and drink. We cold-camped last night and it rained,' he said, indicating a soaking cloak, tied behind his saddle.

Every eye studied him. 'Do we look like Britons?' he asked reasonably.

They did not, they were both clean-shaven and their clothes, although drab were also neat and tidy. Both wore the short-cropped hair of the Saxon, in which not one louse dared to try and live.

'Dismount and enter. You are welcome, but we have to be careful,' one of the men said. 'Slaves, see to these animals right away. I am called Bernic, and this is my friend Arbogastus, who is in a trading partnership with me. We have our two homes close together for mutual defence, as we have our women and children with us. I am sorry we appeared hostile to start with,' Bernic told him as they strolled through the now open gate.

He was a short stout man, while his partner was the direct opposite. Together they appeared to be the long and short of it, which secretly tickled Cenberht's sense of humour. He flashed a look at Crida and was surprised to see the same thought showing. Perhaps Crida was not quite as dumb as he had originally thought.

Of the two of them, Arbogastus was of distant Roman origin, Cenberht thought. He had the very dark colouring and long pointed nose of that race, whereas Bernic was Saxon through and through from his strutting little walk to his quick way of speaking.

56

They were taken into the first house, which belonged to Bernic, and it was a typical Saxon home with a large hall and little rooms leading off. In the main hall lived the family with the sleeping cubicles on one side and a giant cooking fire at the far end. There were fresh reeds underfoot, and the interior was clean and tidy.

Bernic led them to a trestle table, and very quickly a female slave brought hot meat laid on bread platters and good ale to drink.

'My wife Julie will be absent, as she is near her birthing time, and the other women attend her. Drusilla, my partner's wife is also with her.'

'Do you have a son?' Cenberht asked gently. It was always helpful to have information upon every subject.

Bernic shook his head. 'Two daughters so far, though one is sickly, and I doubt she will live much longer. I am hoping the gods will be kinder to me this time, but—' He shrugged, trying to be noncommittal and failing completely. 'I must take what I get.' He eyed his partner. 'He has three sons already!'

Cenberht did not miss the note of envy. Although these two settlers and partners appeared to have easy familiarity between them, it was possible Bernic was the leader. He seemed the more bouncy and go-ahead type. His ear caught the bleat of some sheep and, weighing up what he had already seen, he guessed this was a lucrative settlement. There would be ample water from a stream he had also spotted and fuel enough from the forest.

Crida sat in silence, as befitted his role of servant. He appeared to be utterly relaxed but every nerve was alert with wariness. It seemed to be safe here, where there were women and children, and the two settlers were affable enough, but long ago Crida had learned never to drop his guard.

'So you are a clerk?' Bernic prodded.

Cenberht turned to him pleasantly. He was replete, and after the ale would love to go and sleep it off somewhere, but a guest had duties, as well as those expected of a host. 'I am also looking at land,' he said and nodded around in general. 'I like what I see here, but I intend to ride further northwards and look around there.'

'Be careful then!' Arbogastus warned in a heavy voice. 'Especially if you go north of Bath into that tribal land. They are a very restless lot, and I don't trust them!'

Cenberht pretended to ponder this gem of information. 'Pity,' he drawled. 'I had heard that Gloucester and Cirencester were busy places for the Britons, and I thought if I lived in their territory, paying tribute of course, I could trade with them and their two main tuns.'

'Cirencester is their capital, and you can certainly trade, but I'm not so sure about living so deep in their land. We are all right here. They don't bother us too much, though periodically they swoop and search around. They even tried to come in here but I soon stopped that. They have some hot-headed warriors, especially a large redheaded devil called—' He hesitated and snapped his fingers.

'Melwas!' Arbogastus supplied the name. 'And don't forget that Bracha!'

Cenberht memorised the names. 'Melwas?' he asked interrogatively.

'A bad-tempered, foul-mouthed warrior who is seeking to pick a fight with Saxons. Someone will take him out one day, and it might not be us either. I don't think his own people like him all that much. And Bracha? She is the local chief's daughter and is another hothead too. Always has the reply, and not always with manners either. I expect she is one of those only children who have been allowed to grow up as spoiled brats.' Bernic snapped.

'There is trouble brewing as well,' Arbogastus said with a long face.

Cenberht gave him his full attention. 'What makes you say that?'

Bernic spoke for him. 'A pack train came through only last week on its way to London. They stopped here to barter for two more horses. They said that the tribe in the area north of Bath was extra restless, with many people riding all over the place. The traders were very glad to leave their territory.'

Cenberht stored this away in his mind. It was obvious there was something going on with the Britons, and he was equally certain this was important information for his father.

'What is our king doing? What is his plan?' Bernic asked next.

Cenberht threw him a wry smile. 'I am afraid a humble clerk like me is not one to be privy to royal plans!' he said with a disarming smile.

Crida was a little more relaxed now. His instincts confirmed they were safe here, and he had been admiring Cenberht's smooth way with words and the information he was acquiring. It had dawned upon him that his companion had a very clever mind and glib tongue to go with it.

Cenberht allowed himself the luxury of an open yawn. He could not really help it. The heat from the fire combined with their refreshment, plus a bad night's sleep in the open the previous evening, all helped to make him genuinely exhausted.

Bernic sprang to his feet with an apologetic smile. 'Come to the guesthouse, both of you!' he told them and led the way. 'It's only small, but it's comfortable and you'll have more peace there than in this noisy hall.'

Both Cenberht and Crida knew this was very true, because a sleeping hall was a very noisy place indeed. Perhaps one day someone would invent a place to sleep away from the general living quarters . . .

The next morning, the settlers took their guests to the open gate. 'Don't ride too far west. There is a great river that floods the lowlands. It is all useless for settlement and around Bath is the opposite—extra hilly. You want to pick a place in between—if the Britons will let you!' he ended dryly.

They rode away in a gentle trot but once well away from ears slowed to a walk. 'That was profitable,' Cenberht said, and nodded his head sagely.

'You were very good last night,' Crida told him generously. 'I could not have chatted those two up like you did!'

Cenberht threw him a grin. 'My father says I don't talk enough.'

Now Crida smiled and instantly his craggy lined face was transformed, then he became serious and eyed the sky. The sun was weak, and there were high clouds coming up from the West. 'Do you know the way?'

Cenberht did. He had studied a very ancient map and committed it to memory. 'We head that way, and miss Bath, because we would learn nothing there. Let us head deep into this tribal land and be done with it.'

Crida turned something over in his mind. 'Do you think the Britons suspect our king's intentions?'

Cenberht nodded firmly. 'They are bound to. They are not fools. Also, you can bet they have someone planted among our people, who will, when the time comes, sneak back to report. Perhaps also they have shrewd leaders, who can think and plan ahead.'

Crida knew this meant the Britons could be exceedingly hostile to anyone entering their territory right now. He gulped a little, and it did cross his mind to wonder if the king knew he had sent them both on what might be a suicide mission.

The nature of the land had changed slightly, with more trees around, but no forest. The land rose higher and higher, and, to one side, they could smell habitation—the odours from cooking fires and others more unpleasant from latrines. It was obviously Bath.

They rode along what they knew had to be an old Roman road, but it was badly neglected, covered with weeds, grasses, and in some places even young saplings. Parts of the once fine road were broken and it was crumbled at its edges but they still made fairly easy progress.

At the top of the hill they dismounted to breathe their horses, and look around. There was excellent visibility on this lovely spring day, and they could see for miles. Many plumes of smoke arose from the cooking fires of Bath. Ahead stretched mile upon mile of treetops, but both of them knew this was deceptive. These trees did not indicate a thick, impassable forest. Hidden among them would be clearings, vils and even overnight camps. What appeared to be empty, devoid of human life might, in reality be quite the opposite.

'We will ride straight ahead, and I bet it won't be long before we are spotted!' Cenberht commented dryly.

Crida felt his nerves tighten. This was the enemy's territory. Would his cover as a clerk's escort be believed? He studied his companion, who appeared not to have a care in the world, which meant he was either a brilliant actor or a dumb fool. Crida knew the latter was not the case. There was nothing complacent or the dreamer about the king's son now. He was another person and Crida was very impressed.

They saw no one and made no attempt to hide themselves. Just before dusk Cenberht pointed. 'Let's camp there for the night. We have the provisions Bernic gave us!'

'We'll stand watches though,' Crida growled. 'That will be natural against wild animals without a large fire!' He had no intention of relaxing his guard. He had a itch in the middle of his back, which he was sure came from an observing pair of very hard Briton's eyes.

FIVE

Bracha understood in a flash, faster than the others, even Ygraine. This was a runaway slave who had come to grief in the wilds and was now dying. She doubted whether he would see the day out and there was only one humane way to act. He must be put from his misery at once.

Gandar read her mind. 'Shall I?'

Bracha gave a slow nod. 'It is kinder!'

Ygraine jumped between them. 'No, you won't! I repeat, *I found him!* That makes him mine and you'll not touch him!' she screamed.

'But—!' Bracha began. She could see only too well what Ygraine the healer had in mind. Take him back, care for him but this boy was too far gone.

'Don't you but me, Bracha!' Ygraine shouted, then her hand flew to her knife. 'If either of you go near him my knife will be in your guts. Finders—keepers!'

Her brother was not amused. 'Some find when you scream like that!' he told her tartly. He agreed with Bracha.

Ygraine faltered. 'That was just the shock,' she told them a little lamely but still kept her knife ready for an upper cut attack.

Bracha took a deep breath, suddenly conscious of her position in life and

64

responsibilities. She became deadly serious. 'I will talk to him and my decision will be final. If it is disease—he dies!' she stated flatly and now it was a chief who spoke. Gandar was impressed, Ygraine felt a flutter of fear. This was a strange, new and rather frightening Bracha. If it was disease, the elders would not hesitate to slaughter. Nothing could be risked by the majority for one. Disease was always dreaded in a vill.

Bracha knelt by the boy but kept a prudent distance away while she examined him carefully.

He had no rash. He did not feel hot though his breathing was ragged. There were sweat beads on his forehead but this might be from fear.

'I am Bracha, acting chief of our tun. Who are you?' she asked gently, hoping he could understand. Most slaves could manage a variety of languages.

He replied hesitantly, only too well aware what was at stake. He gave a little gulp and felt tears prickle his eyes. He had already wet himself from shock and fright. He gathered the last dregs of strength to explain himself.

'My name is Hoel, lady!' he started nervously.

'Go on!' Bracha encouraged,

'My lady Januaria has been raped, then killed with her daughter. My master Decius Gaius was killed with all the slaves and servants. The villa was torched, the cattle and other stock let loose, and there was nothing left at all. I was able to hide in the gardens and didn't know what to do. I was very afraid. It was the only home I had known, because they told me I was born there. So I just ran and ran and ran—' and his voice tailed off with a hysterical crack.

Bracha nodded to herself. It was a reasonable story and typical of barbarian activity. It would be easy enough to send out scouts to check. She told herself the story was too simple to be invented. Liars always made their yarns too complicated. Her father had taught her that.

'Why didn't you run to Bath?'

His tears flowed freely now. 'I know many of the Romanos had moved there for safety, but I just panicked. I became lost. I was afraid of the wild animals. I've had nothing to eat, and I began to feel a bit unwell. I began to cough and sneeze—then you found me.'

Bracha considered thoughtfully. It sounded like a plain case of cold and starvation. There was no disease present. She stood and felt Ygraine's eyes boring into her back. 'Take him. He is yours but still keep him isolated—in case!' she said with heavy meaning.

Ygraine's breath came out with a rush of relief and immediately her mind turned to practicalities. 'How?'

Good question, Bracha thought and turned

to Gandar. 'You ride back and get help!'

He was shocked. 'Out of the question! I am not leaving you two alone!'

'Rubbish! There are no enemies here!' Bracha snapped back. The last thing she could put up with was an obdurate Gandar. What had started as a lovely morning away had turned into a mass of problems. 'Very well, I'll go!'

'Definitely not!' Gandar snapped, getting annoyed. 'We have to stay together. Get him up behind me on my horse and tie him on!'

Ygraine looked down. Did he have the strength for this? Hoel had just managed to understand the problem. The fact that he was going to be helped gave him a little extra rush of strength and he staggered to his feet. 'I think I can manage,' he told them hopefully.

Gandar mounted his horse, then, with Ygraine and Bracha pushing and shoving, they were able to double bank him. Bracha was more than a little worried at what the elders would say to this. Gandar eased his mount into a gentle walk, and they started off back home.

Gandar was not at all pleased at the whole exercise. He knew his sister only too well. Once she fell into one of her healing moods she could become very passionate and downright argumentative. What was one runaway slave? He would not have a shred of value, though he supposed moodily if Ygraine could heal him, he might get a small sum if sold. Sold? That would never happen now, if Ygraine had her way. This boy of about her own age was about to become an interesting toy to his sister. He foresaw great problems looming and was suddenly glad he would not have to make decisions. Bracha was welcome to her position.

They made heavy work of their progress with Ygraine fretting and fuming to get back so she could start work on the boy right away. Bracha rode alongside, ready with a supporting hand. Gandar halted suddenly, feeling distinctly uneasy. It was he who first saw the riders, and he halted sharply, with rising worry gnawing at him.

'Why have we stopped?' Bracha wanted to know.

'Riders and they are not Britons either!' Gandar snapped at her.

Bracha was shocked and instinctively prepared to fight. Gandar was left in a difficult position. He studied the riders very carefully; they were Saxon!

'Who are you? What do you want here?' he growled and wished the boy was not behind him. He could see that one of the riders was most definitely civilian but the other was a different matter entirely. He was a trained fighter and looked very competent.

Bracha also kept her eyes on the fighter, then let them drift to close on those of the civilian. As she did so, she was barely able to stifle a gasp of shock. The face that looked back at her was the most handsome she had ever seen and she locked onto very kind eyes that regarded her with considerable interest and not a little amusement.

Cenberht was perfectly well aware of the effect his stunning good looks could have upon all the members of the opposite sex, yet he suddenly realised he was startled. The girl who faced him could never be described as beautiful, yet there was an aura about her, which made him hold his breath with amazement. She sat on her horse with considerable dignity as if she were regal. He could see she was high born, and he did not miss how her weapons sat comfortably upon her body, with one hand resting just a little too casually against her sword hilt. What colour were her eyes? He could not make up his mind and continued to stare deep into them. Fascinated and wordless for once . . .

Bracha felt her heart throb and knew something eerie passed from her to him in a flash, then was held as if knotted. He appeared to have a good body too, and she liked his demeanour. It was upright, open and honest, and she felt drawn to him in a weird and uncanny way, which disturbed her equilibrium.

Gandar and Crida watched each other warily: much too busy sizing each other up as fighters to be aware of the instant magnetism that had flown between the two others. Only

Ygraine remained concerned solely with the boy who was to be her patient, oblivious to anything else. She studied him carefully, and he looked into her eyes. He was weak, but grateful. He had warmed up a tiny bit against the other man's body, but he felt so dreadfully hungry and hoped they would soon arrive at wherever was intended.

'Do hurry up, brother!' she complained fretfully. 'We must get back quickly!'

Gandar continued to glare at Crida who reciprocated in full. Cenberht pulled his eyes away from the girl and rapidly assessed their situation.

'I am a travelling clerk, and this man is my escort. I come in great peace and would like permission to study a little of the land around here with a view to one day perhaps making a settlement for myself. I would wish to become a trader,' he parroted away, not in the slightest bit interested now. Who was this girl? How could he get to know her better? How did the Britons go about allowing a girl and boy to meet? He felt thin ice under his feet so made himself look at their fighter. Not that he could do much right now with someone sitting behind him, who was obviously unwell.

Both Crida and Gandar continued to bristle at each other, rather like two dogs walking very stiff-legged around an inner circle with a bone in the middle.

'Crida!' Cenberht cried, and his cracking

70

voice disturbed both of the fighters.

Bracha realised in a flash this was a dangerous situation. 'Gandar! We must get home!'

Ygraine writhed with impatience. 'For goodness sake, let's move!'

Bracha seized the initiative again. 'Ride with us to our home!' she invited. It was impossible to let him ride out of her life.

Cenberht understood with natural empathy, and he pushed his horse alongside hers and gave a nod of his head to Crida to bring up the rear. He knew he simply could not continue riding through this land, until he had found out more about this fascinating girl, king's orders, or no king's orders.

Bracha thrilled inside, but managed to maintain an aloof exterior dignity, but only with a huge effort. Inside, she bubbled with excitement at the close proximity of this wonderful Saxon. From where had he come? She must learn something about him. She could not let him vanish from her life. What was this which flowed between them? He felt it too. She knew that instinctively. Her heart hammered at her ribs as they rode the last short distance to the vill. As they approached, Gandar emitted an unusual trilling whistle of warning. It was to alert the guard that the strangers, although Saxon, were not entering as hostiles.

They rode into the open clearing and were

immediately the centre of attention. Elesa stared with astonishment but her friend Mona, standing by her side, said nothing, although her eyes were everywhere. She assessed this unusual situation in one calculating glance, then rested on Ygraine's ardent expression. She noted Bracha's more stolid one, yet why did her eyes glow like that? Gandar was obviously on edge, and so was the strange warrior. The only one who appeared totally unconcerned was the strange young man, whose eyes would keep straying to Bracha. She was also sensitive enough to feel waves of something electric, which flowed between them. One eyebrow elevated in deep interest.

'Who the hell are these two? They are the enemy!' Melwas snarled, appearing from his home. He was not a tall man but he was huge across the shoulders and was generally heavily built. Bracha made a snap judgement. Melwas was off his horse in a flash and getting ready to advance with drawn sword. Instantly there was tension.

'Melwas!' she barked and jumped forward to place herself between the two men. 'These strangers are here as guests. My guests. The chief's guests!' and her voice was very cold and penetrating. She was aware all eyes was on her, especially those of the Elders. She rested her hand on the hilt of her sword with a deliberate open gesture.

'They are Saxons!' Melwas repeated in a

snarl and moved as if to push her aside. Instantly Bracha drew her sword and pressed its point into his rather fat belly.

Melwas came from Viking stock. He knew he was both hated and feared by the vill's inhabitants. He did not care about the former and revelled in the latter, because he was both natural bully and sadist.

Crida was usually a controlled, disciplined warrior, but this situation was one he detested. His temper rarely rose but, when it did, he too could become fearsome. He had his sword ready, recognising that which faced him—a loud mouth, but one who could also fight.

'Swine!' he hurled back.

Melwas turned red, hardly able to believe his ears. No one ever called him names. 'Why I'll—!'

Bracha knew she had to break this up. She gritted her teeth, flashed a quick look at the other Saxon, then pressed meaningfully with her sword's tip. It pierced the flesh of Melwas and a little trickle of blood showed. He turned a baleful glare on Bracha, aware of everyone's stillness, then to his surprise and great shock, he read something in the girl's eyes that he immediately understood. She was a killer, after all. He narrowed his eyes and knew he had to back down. He turned on his heel and stamped away in a cold rage, thoroughly humiliated, vowing one day he would have a reckoning.

'I apologise about that, my Lady,' Cenberht

73

said smoothly. 'I can assure you such a situation will not happen from my man again,' and he threw a very hard look at Crida.

Crida watched the big man disappear and nodded sagely to himself. That was certainly not the end of the matter. Well, that was all right with him. He had never ducked a fight in his life, and certainly would not now, with that loudmouth, bullying Briton.

'Bracha, the boy!!' Ygraine shrilled, not in the slightest bit interested in this by-play. 'Someone help me get him down to the little hut over there. I can't lift him on my own, and he's not diseased,' she hastened to add, but no one hurried to help.

Bracha took a deep breath of exasperation. 'You, you and you! Jump to it!' she ordered crisply. 'Well get on with it then!'

She turned to her mother and Mona, smiling at one and ducking her head politely at the other for the moment. 'Can you show these two men the guesthouse please, while I report to the Elders?'

It had taken her considerable effort to remain calm, and keep control of the crisis which had unfolded before her. Gradually, most of the people dispersed, talking animatedly, so she went over to the Elders, sat before them and explained what had happened.

Alun, Cador and Ulfin, the only Elders present just then, were more impressed than

74

they intended to show. Especially Alun. Not once had she raised her voice, bullied or shrieked, yet how quick had been her reaction towards Melwas! Her stock had gone up in his eyes, because it was high time someone sorted Melwas out. He was really neither use nor ornament to any of them.

'As long as the boy does not carry disease he can stay until he recovers. Then we will sell him on. We have our full quota of slaves, since Calthus came. You will be expected to make Ygraine see sense,' Alun told her firmly, knowing just how difficult her friend could be when she was healing a creature, whether it had two legs or four. It would be interesting to see how Bracha handled her friend. 'As to the Saxon guests their time here will be very limited—under the circumstances!' he added pointedly.

Bracha understood and knew Ralf would have the same opinion. In a couple of days, they would be expected to go. She was relieved that her first report had been so well received. She felt quite pleased with herself, but kept her features impassive. She bowed again politely and wandered back to her home. All she could think of, deep down, was the Saxon. How could she strike up a conversation that would appear normal? His escort would be bound to dog his every step.

She saw Ygraine hurtle into the little hut they kept for sick people. She saw Mona walk slowly towards the hut, so, taking a deep breath, she walked to the guesthouse, called out very loud and entered when invited.

Cenberht seemed to be delighted to be here, which puzzled Crida. He had grave reservations that they would be allowed any more than two days here, the normal guest invitation, and to explore deeper into this territory would be most imprudent. So why did his companion look so joyful?

Cenberht moved towards her. 'I am called Cenberht,' he said in a low voice, as their eyes met and spoke for their tongues. He slowly reached out and took one of her hands as something emotionally hard hit his stomach.

Bracha stood rooted to the spot, unable to tear her eyes from his. Crida flashed a look at both, rolled his eyes skywards and wondered what fresh calamity this was going to bring. Young love, sudden love, stupid love, he told himself scornfully, and, worst of all, enemy love. He had a sudden ominous feeling and an emotional chasm yawned before his feet.

'I am Bracha, the chief's daughter, standing in for him while he is—visiting,' she ended with hasty improvisation.

Cenberht saw Crida go outside. It would not do for the two of them to be in a hut alone together. 'Shall we look at the horses?' he suggested meaningfully.

Bracha understood. There were times when her people could be very narrow-minded sexually. 'Follow me and I'll show you where they are!' she offered. What was this buzzing in her head? She had once drunk too much ale and had a similar peculiar feeling. Was it his presence that was making her emotionally drunk? Whatever it was, she had no objections at all.

They walked together, where the horse herd was kept near a small stockade for the night. It had stout fencing and they leaned against this, eyes riveted on one another.

'Is this as alone as we can hope to be?' Cenberht asked in a low voice.

Bracha nodded. 'Who are you really?'

'I was going to ask you the same thing. I feel as if you have bewitched me from the second my eyes landed on you. Are you magic?'

Bracha realised they were both in the same state of emotional upset, and she was very honest. She did not have it in her to play a subterfuge game. 'I feel—!'

'Go on!' he encouraged.

Bracha shook her head. 'I don't have the words. I have never felt like this before, for any other man. As soon as I saw you it was as if you are the one for whom I have been waiting for a very long time,' she whispered, with honesty.

He was almost speechless. His eyes opened wide with shock. 'But that's exactly how I feel!' he marvelled.

'But we are enemies, or at least our peoples

77

are!'

Cenberht yearned to open his heart to her with complete honesty, but was pulled with the tug of filial loyalty. He was acutely conscious his king had entrusted him with a mission of the utmost importance, and he knew he must keep faith or not to be able to live with himself. He gave a groan and gritted his teeth. There was also the offer the king had made for Eadgifu, and he let out a heavy sigh.

Bracha knew instinctively that this was the one male, for her. If she did not have him she would have none. She wanted to reach out, to touch him, to put her head on his chest, to kiss him, but she did not dare do a thing. 'We have only just met!'

Cenberht was sure. He knew that for some few, very lucky people, love could strike at the most outlandish times in impossible situations. 'My father has made an offer for me elsewhere. I don't care for the girl, and don't even know what she thinks about me. Certainly I don't want her now. If I am to wed and to mate, it is with you only. It is a destiny. I never thought when I set out on this trip—' and his words tailed away wonderingly.

Bracha understood. 'When I arose this morning it was just another ordinary day. I never thought it could turn out to be the most wondrous day of my life. What can we do? It's like a madness! A courtship takes weeks! Not just a few hours!'

They looked at each other, so incredibly in tune with one another that speech was hardly necessary. Each knew their life would never be the same again and if they were parted permanently it would be too horrific to contemplate.

They both became aware that Calthus had come back, and was only a few paces away, staring at them with amazement, his eyes on a glittering blue ornament, which hung from a gold chain around Cenberht's neck. Cenberht turned slowly and gave the slave a hard, cool stare. Calthus flushed and went about his business though his heart pounded.

Cenberht made up his mind. 'I know this is crazy. It is almost a midsummer madness, but I also know my mind. There will never be any female for me—but you. Will you wear my troth?' he asked her anxiously.

She never hesitated. 'Yes, I will, and with great pride as well!' she gulped and thought rapidly, then, with slightly trembling fingers, unfastened her brooch, palmed it, then slid it into his hand. His fingers clasped it, while his heart throbbed with emotion, and, at the same time, taking a peek around to make sure they were not observed, he slid the gold chain and pendant from his neck. 'Wear it as my troth but you'd better keep it hidden for a bit,' he advised wisely.

She flipped it over her head and passed the jewel under her tunic before fastening the top toggle to hide the chain from view. They looked at each other and grinned wildly, both highly pleased with themselves and their cleverness.

'Is there no chance for us to be alone?' he asked wistfully.

She shook her head sadly. 'And you will only be able to stay two nights here at the most. It's because you're Saxons,' she explained sadly.

Cenberht stifled a groan of frustration. He knew he had gone mad, he acknowledged that, but by all the gods, what a wonderful insanity it was. 'I'll go back roughly the way I came to my home tun but then I'm going to come back and get you. I don't know how or when, but I'll be back for you. You will wait for me?' he asked anxiously.

Bracha felt his sudden fear. 'Yes, I give you my oath upon that, we have plighted our troth. No one will agree with us. They will all say it's sudden insanity and we will be scorned. But I don't care!' she vowed.

His face brightened. 'My sentiments exactly. We live our lives, as we want and not as others expect. You might perhaps hear things about me—' he started picking each word with great care, '—but don't believe all that which you might hear. My oath is also for you, and nothing and no man will make me change my mind!' he vowed in his turn.

Bracha was puzzled. 'I don't understand?'

'I cannot explain more just now. Family

problems,' he continued heavily. 'Just remember that I will be back to claim you!'

It entered Bracha's head that he must mean the coming war but, all of a sudden, she had lost complete interest in it all and the Saxons in general. She was interested in only one Saxon in particular. Was he a spy? Her instinct told her that he was but she no longer cared. She realised she was being totally and utterly selfish and, for the first time in her life, she did not give a damn.

SIX

Bracha opened the door to the sick room and halted, reeling with the heat. Inside Ygraine had a huge fire roaring and Bracha was stunned. 'How can you stand this?'

Ygraine looked up at her. She was exhausted. She had been up all night with the slave and her eyes were red-rimmed but glowed with triumph. 'It's working!' she said.

'What is?' Bracha gasped, shoulders sagging. It was unbearable.

'I'm sweating the sickness from him. He's had some broth and kept it down. I also made an inhalation and listen to how much better his breathing is.'

Bracha studied the slave. He lay on a paliasse, covered with an animal pelt and his face was scarlet. Although he sweated profusely, his breathing was steadier and minus the horrible bubbling sounds. Ygraine had stripped him, just tossing a small fur over his genitals under the larger one and she now pulled the latter away.

Bracha saw a lean body, far too thin, but it was nothing that good food would not cure. He was fairly free from scars, and she wondered about his back. Ygraine read her mind. 'He has never been flogged,' she said in a low voice.

Did that mean he was spiritless or just more cunning than anyone else in his position? It was a pity, the elders would not keep him as he was of good breeding age but they were correct. They could only support so many slaves so he would have to be sold on, and how would Ygraine react to that? Bracha did not like to consider.

Hoel opened his eyes and looked up at the stern lady. He gave a little gulp and tried to half-sit so Ygraine began to fuss.

Bracha waved with one hand. 'Tell me your story again,' she invited. He told it word for word, and she knew he had told the truth. 'Do you have any hopes in life?'

Hoel was astounded. Slaves as mere two-legged animals were not supposed to have feelings about anything, let alone hope. He thought for a moment, then nodded a little shyly. 'I would like to own coins to buy my freedom,' he said tentatively.

Bracha nodded thoughtfully. 'Can you use any weapons? Have you been trained?'

Hoel nodded. 'I have been taught how to use spear and dagger, but that is all. I want to learn more. If I could fight, and I would give my allegiance and—'

'A slave does not have an allegiance so cannot give one!' Bracha rebuked.

Ygraine bridled at her harshness. 'Bracha!' she protested . . .

Bracha ignored her as she lay down some ground rules. Why she did this, she had no idea, but something prodded at her. 'As a slave cannot give allegiance so he cannot give an oath of loyalty, because he doesn't have an oath in the first place,' she continued remorselessly. 'This also means he can have no honour!'

Hoel had recovered enough to be stung into protest. 'That's not fair, Lady I do have honour and loyalty especially to those who have let me live!'

Good, Bracha told herself. He is bright enough to get my drift. Ygraine missed it all, which only meant she was now so besotted with her patient she had lost her wits. Then she saw a tender curve to Ygraine's lips, and a gentle glow in her eyes. This is a double madness, she told herself. There had to be a mischievous spirit about, because it was obvious now that Ygraine's feelings were more than an obsession. Inwardly, she groaned. Ygraine in love with a slave? This was impossible. The implications and complications were too enormous for her to contemplate at that moment.

'Just concentrate on getting well and strong!' she said kindly and, standing, looked deep into her friend's eyes, yet Ygraine did not even see her.

She walked away and strolled down to the horses. It was his last day here, and her heart slumped.

Calthus held Cenberht's horse, while he checked its legs. Crida stood respectfully back, looking around in general, and then he saw the chief's daughter coming over. He had already made some astute deductions regarding the female and his companion. The conclusion at which he had arrived did not make healthy reasoning. If Cenberht and this Bracha had done something so crazy as to fall in love after only a few hours the sky was going to drop down on them when the king knew. Crida had no intention of being in the vicinity of what would be the mother and father of all storms.

Cenberht bent his head so that it was against that of the slave as if he too wished to look at the horse's leg. 'You know who I am?'

'Yes, sir, and thank all the gods you have come. I could not have put up with much more of this!' Calthus confided in a low whisper. He had been staggered to see the openly displayed

84

pendant, though why it had been passed to the girl was beyond him. Surely she was not part of this as well? She was the chief's daughter, a bossy little madam as well. 'I have been demeaned and humiliated beyond words especially when the king arranged for me to be sold by those Romanos!!'

Cenberht was disinterested in listening to a lot of complaints. The king could handle those. 'Do you have all the information the king can possibly want?'

Calthus saw the chief's daughter coming. 'You are getting a visitor, so we'll have to be quick,' he warned. 'I have everything in my head. The main point is that the British kings have done the unthinkable. They have united, and they will have a very large force of men to face us. They have already chosen the battle site, at a place called Deorham.'

Cenberht was staggered with this information. Then he turned to practicalities. 'Are you guarded at night or free to roam? I intend to leave when it is dark. I hope you can ride with us. You have been a very great man, and done a wonderful job!'

'I am not guarded but I'm with two others, and I've no weapons except my dagger.'

'Try and get some ale to get the other two drunk. Make sure you stay very sober. There will a good moon tonight. Check our horses are well fed and watered and pick a good one for yourself, then stay alert until we can slide out and join you. Crida will knock out the sentry. We will leave here, very quietly then ride like hell for home by the shortest possible route. There will be a chase after you and us once they realise we are together. So no stopping anywhere, if we can help it. We must avoid the settlers because that is the first place they will want to check. Our settlers are strong enough and well armed enough to protect themselves. Our job and our duty is to get the information back to the king as quickly as possible. Hello Bracha! How lovely to see you again!' and Cenberht did not lie. He was just so thankful he had managed to gabble out all the necessary instructions in time. All he had to do was prime Crida.

Calthus tactfully removed himself, eyed Crida, questioningly, realised he knew nothing and walked away, turning over in his mind the best way to get his night companions drunk, and stay sober himself.

'You'll go soon, won't you?' Bracha asked with a catch in her voice and a horrible lump in her throat.

Cenberht wanted to snatch her in his arms but dared do nothing except stand still and appear to be involved in casual conversation concerning horses.

'Yes, and I can't say any more—for your protection,' he told her heavily. 'Just remember, you are mine and I am yours, and no matter what happens, what you hear or what you see, nothing can change our troth. You have my oath I will be back for you, but I cannot say exactly when. Just be ready for me. Please?' he begged in a husky voice.

Bracha nodded. She knew her father was due back at any time, so it was prudent for her lover to depart rapidly. Her eyes filled with tears, she gave a sniff, nodded, then forced herself to walk away in a totally unconcerned manner. It was the biggest performance of her life. He felt this and was humbled.

Later on in the early evening in the guest house, he told Crida, everything. 'Calthus the slave has always been the king's man. He really is an earldorman from Kent. The king thought up this scheme a long time ago and Calthus was brave enough to volunteer. He has all the possible information needed by the king. It's all stored in his head so our job now is to get him back as quickly as possible, and intact. You see, I was sent here deliberately to get him out!'

Crida was stunned at the simplicity and daring. This plan had been brilliant in its boldness, and he could only marvel at the cunning of King Ceawlin to have thought it out. And the remarkable daring and heroism of a man in allowing himself to be sold into slavery. He knew he could never have done this. The planning involved, the sheer risk for Calthus, had been enormous. His heart swelled with pride to be a member of the

Saxon race. The Britons had no chance at all against such mental brilliance.

'We'll have to ride like maniacs, and the king knew this. So for a number of days, very well armed patrols will have been crossing the frontier, awaiting our return, which I'm sure is going to be at top speed!' he said dryly.

Crida gave a delicate little cough, went to speak, turned scarlet and changed his mind. Cenberht outguessed him. He gave him a gentle smile and looked into the distance of the wooden walls for a few seconds.

'I love her! She loves me! We are betrothed, and nothing and no man, which includes a king, can stop us!'

Crida looked at him sympathetically. Did he really think he was powerful enough to stand up against and browbeat King Ceawlin? He gave a tiny shake of his head in sorrow. And what about the girl? She was the daughter of a chief. He had a sudden knowledge she was going to be in the same position. How blind, how foolish, how short-sighted was young love?

Mona missed nothing. Long ago she had developed the art of moving silently and unobtrusively and had often nearly given a night sentry a heart attack. She had positioned herself at the side of a house, in shadow where she could be hidden but watch with interest. Her attention had been riveted on the interplay between the Saxon and the chief's daughter. She was not shocked. She was only too well aware of the awesome power of young, hot blood. It was but the natural call of nature when like magnetised like in the age-old mating game. It was quite unstoppable and she understood because once, she too, so long ago, had been held enthralled by another.

She had seen the difference in the girl that responsibility had given and she had approved. The Saxon, a total stranger from another race, had fascinated her. She had studied him intently—not just for his looks but his whole demeanour and general attitude. He was young but had an assurance and natural confidence that impressed. His manners were impeccable, which showed he was well bred and she guessed he had a keen, well-formed intellect.

She moved forward as Bracha appeared obviously to walk down to the guesthouse in which were the two Saxons. Mona showed herself and made Bracha start with surprise then the old lady nodded pointedly at the guesthouse. Bracha was quick to understand, and she called his name.

Cenberht appeared, saw the two onlookers and halted uncertainly. Mona stepped forward and stared hard into the Saxon's eyes. He bore her gaze without flinching, and held it. Mona gave him a smile of approval, turned to Bracha, grasped her right hand, and drew her forward.

Looking at both of them, in turn, with her steady penetrating eyes she clasped their right hands together and squeezed encouragingly. 'It is going to be hard. Very hard!' she warned each in turn. 'If you can survive what is to be, then no one will ever divide you!' she told them in a soft, low voice.

Bracha and Cenberht looked at each other, then back to the old woman. They stood in a little personal tableau of three from which the rest of the world was totally excluded.

Mona felt great pity rise up in her for the couple. They simply had no idea of the trauma to come, and she knew she would witness the unfolding events with enormous interest. She gave one final squeeze of the two hands, then broke their clasp, spun Bracha around and pushed her away, then nodded at the Saxon to get back inside the guesthouse. As she had personally made the human tableau, now she took it upon herself to shatter it.

Finally, as if she had done an enormous human duty, Mona moved back to her original position deep in complicated thought. She knew that Ralf would soon have to return as she also knew Elesa failed to see or understand. Because of all these complications, Mona decided to spend a few more days with these people before she moved off to face the inevitable.

Bracha's feelings were confused and perplexed by Mona's strange behaviour, although she was glad the old lady had realised where two hearts lay. But what had she meant by her strange sentences? If only these wise old Druidic trained people could speak without tangling everything up in mysterious riddles.

Ygraine burst into sight, spotted her friend and hurried over. She grabbed one arm and pulled her to one side for some privacy.

'He's better!' Ygraine gushed. 'I knew I could cure him. Come and see for yourself!'

Bracha felt a silent scream rise. *I want to be alone with my thoughts!*

She allowed Ygraine to drag her back to the sick hut, though her heart was throbbing to breaking point. She knew instinctively that tonight he would be going. He would not wait for the daylight, because then he would be too easy to follow or ambush. Why had Mona uttered those enigmatic words? What did Mona sense, or even know, which was hidden from her?

Ygraine hauled her friend into the house and Bracha was relieved that the temperature was normal. The slave was up and dressed. Bracha was so astonished that she forgot her own problems and worries for the moment. The slave bowed his head to her and, though still skeletally thin and bony, he stood upright, bright and alert. He breathed as easily as herself, and it was obvious Ygraine had succeeded with a wondrous cure. 'Well!' was all she could get out.

'Lady, and I am grateful! I am well now, I would like to stay here and work,' Hoel began. He had rehearsed his words carefully, only too well aware he was still in a precarious position. Officially, he was lost property and morally bound to these people who had saved his life. If they could not find the legal owner they could sell him and pocket his worth in coins themselves. The last thing Hoel wanted was that. He wanted a home. A proper home. Not just any home, but one here. From the moment his thoughts had cleared enough for him to be aware of his surroundings, he had taken to the sounds from outside the sick house. It seemed a happy place, which the Romano villa had not been. He had been glad to work outside, away from harsh domestic blows. He dared to wonder and wish that there might be a chance for him here. He felt gratitude to his nurse. He knew perfectly well he had been sliding rapidly to death, and he was so grateful he would do anything for her. Anything within a slave's limited powers.

Bracha knew this was out of the question. The elders had spoken, and he was to be sold on as surplus to requirements. Surely Ygraine had the wit to see this—or did she? She studied her friend and noted how Ygraine's eyes glowed, and not just with pride at her nursing skill. There was something else mirrored in them, which startled Bracha and made her frown momentarily. She gave a little gasp, as she understood. Ygraine was as besotted as she herself. She was helplessly trapped in the same crazy, emotional madness.

'We'll have to see, Hoel!' she prevaricated, then she threw a hinting look at Ygraine to go outside.

'You've fallen in love with him!'

Ygraine nodded. 'Can't help it. He's all I've ever wanted in a man and you should see the size of his balls. I bet he can make love beautifully!'

Bracha was speechless. This was total madness. Both of them? She bit her lip. 'I understand. Me too with the Saxon!' she confessed.

Now it was Ygraine's turn to marvel. 'What do we do?'

Bracha gave a heavy shrug. 'I have to explain to my father when he does return—' and then the sentence tailed off uneasily. 'As to Hoel, he will have to be sold. You know that! Just as you know you cannot buy him and mate with him. He is slave and you are freeborn. And don't get ideas about talking to the elders right now. Alun is in a foul mood with the joint ills and Mona is trying to help him. You ask Alun anything right now, and you'll get an automatic no!' she warned.

'But what can I do?' Ygraine, almost wailed.

'I know. You go and see him and tell him how I feel, and then we might have a better idea how to handle the situation!'

'Oh no!' Bracha protested. 'There is a limit to what friends can do!!'

Ygraine was ready for her. 'But you are the chief right now and it is the chief's duty to see to the welfare of every member of the community. That includes me!'

Bracha knew when she was trapped. 'Blackmailer!' she said, then turned on her heel to walk back into the sick house.

Hoel gave a little jump. He had been standing there marching up and down on the spot, trying to exercise himself a little. He wondered if the marvellous healing lady would come back and talk to him again. He did not expect the chief's daughter, who worried him with her position and sternness.

Bracha halted before him, glowered, then shot it all out undiplomatically. 'Your healer has fallen in love with you. She especially admires your balls. How do you feel about her?'

Hoel was quite staggered. He blinked, his jaw dropped, and his wits left him. He struggled to speak, his tongue tripped then he controlled it, as he went scarlet with embarrassment. 'I hadn't thought about it, Lady,' he managed to get out.

Bracha eyed him moodily. 'That's a lie, if ever I heard one!' she snapped. 'Don't play silly games with me. I'm too busy. Do you or do you not fancy her and not as a healer either?'

'I'm flattered!' and his voice almost squeaked, then he gave her a warm smile. 'She is rather nice though. I think she has beautiful breasts. When she leaned on me I peeped through half open eyes, and—!' His voice tailed off uncertainly.

Bracha stifled a groan. It was Cenberht and she all over again with a vengeance. 'You are just a slave, and the healer is freeborn. The elders plan to sell you in the near future because we have enough slaves for our wants. However, my father should be back any day and I'll see what I can say to him,' she told him and knew it would have to be well before she dared to mention her personal situation. 'Could Mona help?' flashed through her mind. She knew that Mona considered people must work out their own destinies, for better or worse. 'You say you are used to riding animals. In another couple of days, you can go and help with the horses if you feel strong enough. In the meantime, keep exercising here.'

Outside Ygraine went from one foot to the other. 'What did he say?'

Bracha bottled her rapidly rising temper. 'He admires your big breasts, and now I'm going to see my mother!' she ended very pointedly and strode away.

SEVEN

Bracha awoke with a violent start as noise hammered at her. She lay for a few bemused seconds then leapt up. Cenberht was bolting!! She plunged into her clothes. Outside her little cubicle she cannoned into Elesa who was bleary-eyed with shock.

'What's happened?' Elesa shouted. 'Are we under attack from the Saxons?'

Bracha could say nothing but she had started to sweat with fear for him. They were only two men against many, which included Melwas. She flew outside, eyes everywhere in the moonlight. It was pandemonium. Everyone was outside, shouting and bellowing, Melwas noisiest of all, of course. Alun and two other elders had appeared, struggling to make head or tail of the vill's uproar, the hounds had joined in with a cacophony of howling and horses plunged around loose, frightened by the noise.

'Catch the horses!' Alun shouted but that was easier said than done.

'Don't chase them, you fool!' Bracha snarled at Melwas. 'Gentle them!'

Gandar, Ricole, Ygraine and Hoel had all joined in the fray as the horses plunged wildly to get away to total freedom.

'The gate has been opened deliberately!'

Gandar cried, thrusting a rope around one horse's neck who promptly reared.

Hoel ran forward to help without thinking while everyone tried to rope a horse then force a bridle over their heads.

'Where's that horse slave, Calthus?' Melwas raged. 'He wants flogging for allowing this to happen!'

Bracha frowned. Yes, where was Calthus? That was a good question. An idea niggled into her mind. Had he gone with Cenberht and his man and, if so, for what purpose? She stared intently. He was nowhere to be seen. Gradually the loose horses were all restrained and Alun began to jig up and down with rage.

'Get after who did this and bring them back. Dead or alive!' he roared.

Bracha became aware Mona was watching her and she knew she turned scarlet. The old eyes stared at her remorselessly and a smile touched thin lips.

'Clever boy,' Mona whispered, 'but I just hope he can ride hard and fast!' and she nodded to where Gandar, Melwas and others had managed to mount and grab spears.

Bracha was torn: she wanted to ride with them and see Cenberht to safety but knew she dared not. She was badly puzzled. Cenberht had not said he knew anyone in her vill, especially a slave, so why had Calthus vanished as well? Had he just grabbed an opportunity to bolt during the general mêlée? Or was there some deeper, ominous meaning to his disappearance? A heavy weight sank to the bottom of her stomach.

Calthus had been a plant. It would be the easiest thing in the world to persuade some volunteer, with the bait of great wealth and reward, to allow himself to be put into such a position to glean information. Her opinion of King Ceawlin shot up high and, at the same time filled her with sudden dread for the future. What kind of a king was he to make such a subtle plan and to wait patiently? Then there was Cenberht. Who exactly was he? She could see it all now. He had told her a pack of lies to get himself into this site to extract the Saxon spy. She had fallen for it completely, and she gritted her teeth with humiliation.

She knew she wasn't the only one. Everyone had been fooled, but it was she whose heart had been attacked. She swallowed miserably. Could she believe all his statements? Would he come back to her? Or was everything he said false? She knew her vow had been given from the heart, and she would stand by it through thick and thin. But Cenberht? A desperation rose in her. Surely he had meant what he said? Was it simply a task he had to do for the Saxon king, and once he was free he would be back for her?

Gradually, everything was under control again, and riders had departed, chasing the Saxons. Bracha doubted they would catch them in the dark, because obviously this too had been planned in minute detail. People still milled around, gossiping furiously.

Hoel had retreated back to the open door of the sick house. Elesa stood talking with some of the other women. Ygraine was nowhere to be seen at the moment. Mona was present in her usual observing position in the shadows of a house. Bracha smiled at her a little wanly and walked over. She stood before her, the wise old woman, lacking speech, just her eyes huge, sad and worried.

Mona understood only too well. This girl who had been wild and brash was now going through the trauma of pain and worry—those character-forming obstacles, which showed whether the recipient had backbone or not.

'I'm scared!' Bracha confessed and there was a catch in her voice.

Mona plumbed the depths of the girl's soul with years of accumulated wisdom. She said not a word but clasped Bracha's hands in her own, squeezed and looked deep into her eyes.

Bracha managed a rueful, weak smile and Mona nodded approvingly. Once that would have been a scowl or sulk. Mona had started to change her mind and was delighted. Did the girl know that in her pedigree, generations back, she had Druid ancestry? She doubted this and had no intention of telling her. *Yet. A* day in the future would be more opportune when the girl had been through her personal trial by fire.

Bracha saw the dawn was with them and a rather bad-tempered Alun stood and glowered at all of them.

'You come here!' he barked as Bracha hurried over.

'What do you know about this disgraceful affair?'

'Nothing, Alun!'

He gave her a hard scrutiny. 'You spent a lot of time talking to him. I may be old but there's not much wrong with my eyes yet!

Bracha forced herself to keep a straight face and she prayed she did not blush with guilt. 'Just young people's talk,' she floundered, then seeing her mother, waved and walked away, heart thudding. The last thing she could stand would be one of Alun's interrogations.

Alun watched her retreating back, and a small suspicion began to send up a seed of doubt. She was up to something. Bracha had an obvious look of guilt on her face. He opened his mouth to call her back when suddenly Ygraine was before him.

Ygraine burst forth in a torrent of words. 'I know you said you were going to sell Hoel when he is fit, and that he might make a decent price but you can't do that. He is not yours to sell in the first place. I found him, which makes him my property and our laws are quite clear about this. Only I can agree to his sale, and I won't do that. Also you need

100

him now, don't you?' she challenged.

Alun was taken aback, quite unprepared for a verbal onslaught. Ygraine's face flared red, and she was obviously working herself into a female tantrum. He had to admit her reasoning had been sound so far but he had other more important matters to deal with than slave trivialities or giddy young girls. 'See the chief or the acting chief!' he growled coldly. 'I am too busy!'

'No!' Ygraine continued. 'Now that Calthus has gone. We are going to be a slave short here, aren't we?' she questioned sweetly.

Bracha had heard this exchange, because both of their voices had risen to a high and angry pitch. Ygraine was more cunning that she had thought!

'Go away, girl, and don't bother me!' he shouted, and he waved a hand dismissively.

Bracha ran back, snatched her friend's arm and pulled her away. 'He's all bad-tempered. Don't make him worse, for goodness sake!'

Ygraine grinned at her. She was quite happy to turn aside now. She had made her point and in public, which had put Alun on the spot.

'I told you so! He is mine!' she crowed.

Bracha gave in. 'All right, he is yours, and what are you going to do if he decides you are not for him?'

Ygraine's face fell a little. 'But you said—!'

'Ygraine, drop it,' Bracha said wearily. 'I have my own problems, don't forget!'

Bracha became aware of her mother. 'Come in, sit down and have a drink. The uproar has died down a bit and dawn is coming properly.'

It crossed Bracha's mind to wonder if her mother suspected anything. Some of their slaves bustled about seeming to do nothing in particular so Elesa waved a hand and shooed them all away. Mother and daughter sank on low stools before the log fire. Some of the wood was unseasoned and it spat, and sap oozed from under peeling bark.

Bracha took a long pull of ale and was almost unaware of what it was. Elesa regarded her very fondly, but with concern. Nowadays, she had a lot of worry, which she had been keeping to herself. Ralf had always been hot-tempered, but recently he had flared up more often. She also wondered if it was her imagination that he seemed to be getting thin. She had resolved to speak to Mona about these worries but first of all there was Bracha to contend with.

'Do you want to talk about it?' she asked in a gentle voice.

Bracha looked deep into her mother's eyes. She gave a sigh that showed she carried the woes of the world on her back. The words would not come easily, and suddenly she was afraid.

Elesa understood. The opening was left to her and she was glad now Ralf was away. 'Mona has been in to talk to me a little,' she said huskily.

Bracha nearly choked on her drink. 'She has?'

Elesa nodded. 'Are you quite sure about what you plan to do?'

Bracha stalled for time to try and recover from this fresh shock. 'What would that be, Mother?'

'Oh, daughter, don't you think, I don't know what true love is?' Elesa said and smiled softly, at past memories. 'Do you know, long, long ago, I married a fine young warrior. The only trouble was, I did not care for him, but my parents arranged the match. I was so young, and did not stand up for myself. You see, I loved someone else. He was my whole life, and without him I was ready to lie down and die. I put up with the marriage, and in a way, I was lucky. My fine young husband was a lousy hunter and a boar took him twelve months later.'

Bracha sat fascinated. Never before had her mother opened her heart, and she doubted this would have happened now if Ralf had been present. There were times when her father put a damper on the domestic atmosphere. 'What happened then?'

'In that year, my lover had also married when he realised he had lost me, but fate took a strange turn. She died in childbed, and the baby with her, so suddenly we were both free. We were older, wiser, and that much stronger!'

'What did you both do?' Bracha asked with awe.

Elesa grinned. 'Why I married him of course and you came along!'

'Father?'

Elesa smiled. 'I never regretted the wait though I was sorry about it, but we have more than made up for it. So you see, if we had been stronger at the very beginning we would have had that extra time together.'

Bracha turned all this over in her mind, took a deep breath and looked hard into her mother's eyes. 'You know, don't you? I am betrothed to the Saxon Cenberht!'

'So, Mona indicated!' and she paused to select her words with care. 'It seems a bit hurried, but I know true love can be like that. The great problem for you is that he is the enemy! I don't know what your father is going to say,' she warned.

Bracha groaned. 'I know, and I feel rather scared about telling him, especially after this night's work. I did guess the Saxons would go tonight, when it's just about impossible to follow them in the dark. But I did not know about the slave.'

Elesa pulled a face. 'By the time your father does return, he will be totally exhausted, and most likely in a very foul mood,' she warned softly. 'It might be prudent for you to hold your tongue for one or two days.'

'Will Mona tell him?'

Elesa shook her head. 'Mona and me are friends, going back many years ago, she once had her eyes on your father too!'

Bracha was staggered again. 'But she is so much older than you! She must have been old when she fancied father!'

Elesa shook her head. 'Mona is only a handful of years older than me. She looks so much more because of the kind of life she has led, always on the go, moving from tribe to tribe, never a settled home of her own or a man to call her own. That's why, in a way, I have always done my best to share my home life with her. And I have had so much and she has had so little, yet look at the great service she has done to the people as a healer.'

They eyed each other. 'Take it gently with your father!' she advised.

Bracha's jaw set in a pugnacious line. 'He won't make me change my mind!' she said belligerently.

Elesa refrained from comment. There were times when Bracha could still be a little naïve. Experience must be her tutor. Had she forgotten the awesome power of a tun's chief? This was not the most appropriate moment to remind her either. Her heart went out to her daughter and she held her hand. 'Just be quite sure with your heart!' She paused. 'Look at it all again in the cold light of the next dawn!' she advised carefully. 'Remember, there is war on the horizon and warriors die in battle!'

Bracha's heart went cold. This was something she had not even remotely considered. Would Cenberht have to fight against her people? Of course he must! What if they met on the actual battlefield? It was not an impossibility, and her heart plummeted further. 'I'm going to have some fresh air!' she choked and sprang up, stumbling outside, the problems of the world now on her shoulders.

Peace reigned once more and this time with highly alert sentries. Gandar and Melwas had come back from a futile chase and, grouped together with other fighters, were talking about what to do next.

Bracha avoided them, plodding with a sick heart. She hoped she would not bump into Ygraine, because if her friend started on about that slave again, she knew she would stand and scream. To her surprise it was Hoel, who slid from a shadow to accost her.

'Lady,' he began a little nervously. His lips were dry, and his heart fluttered. He was unused to addressing high-ranking people.

'What is it?' Bracha asked wearily.

'The healing lady has gone!' Hoel informed her, and Bracha blinked with surprise. 'She spoke to me before she left!' he added and Bracha was even more astounded. 'She told me to serve you always, because my destiny is tied in with yours and if I obey, and please you, my path in life will work out for me as I want!' he finished in a little flurry of words.

106

For a few moments Bracha was quite speechless. Mona had said all that? It was a speech, not a few words, but why? *'Am I going mad?'* Since when did Mona, talk with anyone—apart from Elesa—let alone give advice in plain words? She eyed Hoel anew. Yes, she thought, he would indeed make a good match for Ygraine but how could he possibly fit into her life's plans? It was all too much for her.

'Thank you,' she replied gently. 'And I will remember!' though what good that would do she had no idea. 'If ever I send for you—?'

Hoel answered before she could finish her sentence. 'I would come instantly, Lady. I am also discreet—even though young,' he said, his sincerity obvious.

Bracha grinned at him as her spirit lightened. 'You'd better go and find your young healer!' she advised. 'She'll want to check up on you!'

Bracha knew she must, she simply must be alone with her very complicated thoughts.

EIGHT

This was a new fear, and it tore at his guts. All through his adult life, fear had been a regular companion, which, when he became mature, he realised was no bad thing for a warrior. The

107

fighter without fear, who charged in without thought, was a hazard to himself and his companions. The warrior with fear in his heart was more skilful, much more alive, extremely alert and with lightning reflexes. The man who said he never knew fear was either a liar or a stupid fool.

There were degrees of fear, and this he had not experienced before, so he had no idea how to work it out. Ceawlin gritted his teeth as the fear slithered around his heart again, and squeezed.

What a fool he had been in the past! He had never appreciated Cenberht, seen his full potential as a son, albeit on the wrong side of the blanket. There were so many times when he had ignored him—not from direct rudeness, but from natural indifference. This son lived, moved around, learned and that was all.

It had taken him a while to come to his senses last year, and understand that only Cenberht would do. Initially, it had been a bitter pill to swallow, and he had even been nervous. What if Cenberht refused? It was certainly a task only for a volunteer, so, during that past winter, he had taken to studying this peculiar son with more attention.

Cenberht definitely was odd. His tutors said it was because he was so bright others were unable to attain his mental plane. Ceawlin had snorted at this, then gradually had to accept his own error. His legitimate son, even when adult would not, he reckoned, have Cenberht's intellect. Cenberht knew the king did not have it either. What he did have, though, was an enormous store of pure guile and animal cunning, rarely matched by any other man.

He could not now remember exactly when the idea had entered his head. It did not come as a flash of inspiration, but developed gradually, enlarging as it took over more and more of his mind. It was crazy the Saxons should be so confined on this island. Expansion was the only answer but, after Artorius, victory had to be very positive indeed.

For this, detailed information was required, but how to get it and then pass it on? It would also require a very special man, one of incredible bravery, considerable courage and superb acting skills. When Ceawlin had looked around, one man after the other had been dismissed, and it was only when he spread his net much wider on a trip to Kent that he met Calthus.

He had not found it too easy to explain his plan but Calthus had listened intelligently. Strangely enough it was the wife of Calthus who came down in his favour, for which he would be forever grateful. She understood the king's point of view, and agreed with it. If her man could do such a fine service what was nine months to a year's separation, provided, of course, the reward at the end would meet her expectations? She had made this very clear, and she had not hummed and hawed about it either. Calthus would enter the nobility as a very high-ranking earldorman.

If the subject had not been so serious, Ceawlin would have been amused at the way the good wife had played him like a fish on a line and so the bargain had been struck. Calthus had quietly slipped away, and his wife had moved nearer to the king for protection as she was childless.

So Ceawlin fretted and fumed for Cenberht's return, getting rather short-tempered in the process. Ethel adored her Calthus and had given him three children, all sons, but not one had lived beyond five years. So now, childless and missing her husband, she had become bored. She was a small, bustling woman and an excellent cook. With no husband and family to look after, she still could not help cooking. Her stew-pot always held the most delicious smells, so naturally, the footloose males had taken to wandering near her home when they calculated that a meal was ready. Ethel was generous. She delighted in filling a man's belly and the worst culprit of all was Cutha.

Cutha had been widowed twice, each time losing his woman in childbed, as happened so often. He had vowed he would never marry again, but take his fun as and when he could snatch it.

There were times when Ceawlin wondered how far Cutha had managed to get with Ethel, then, each time, he dismissed the thought as unworthy of such a good woman. Knowing his brother as he did, he knew it would not be for lack of trying. Cutha had incredible charm when he chose to use it. Ceawlin had made sure Cutha knew nothing of his plans. The only people privy to his idea were the actual participants. Even Cenberht had only been told at the last breathless gasp. This meant Ethel was man-less in Cutha's roving eyes. Ceawlin had issued a few discreet hints that this state was only temporary but the months had passed more quickly than the king had originally calculated.

With Calthus hopefully on his way back, he hoped Cutha would wander elsewhere, with his beseeching eyes and empty belly. There were more than enough female slaves to accommodate him but Cutha, in his own way, also had an awkward streak in his makeup.

Each dawn a patrol went out, commanded by trusted men. Their orders were positive. They were to go over the frontier and wait for two or three men who might be coming in one hell of a hurry, most likely with angry Britons on their heels. They were to fight no more than was necessary to extricate these men, and they should be brought immediately to the king's presence without allowing any of them to be harmed. One would be his son, who would be identification enough. The second would be the dour warrior Crida, and he did not bother to explain whom the third would be.

As day after day went by, Ceawlin's fear and temper rose. His men itched to know what this was all about but even the close nobles dare not question the king or even hint. Cutha was baffled by it all but his brother in one of his foul moods was best left strictly alone.

The king did not say a word to Ethel either. He could not. If anything had happened, and Calthus was dead, then it would be bad enough going to her. To lift up her hopes prematurely would be the height of cruelty. So, the King of the Saxons mooned about his tun, quietly driving everyone mad. He did not ride out. He did not engage in sports. He ignored a weapons' practice, and he even refused to call a council to elucidate his forward planning.

'What the hell is the matter with him?' Cutha mouthed to one of the nobles when a civil question received a vile answer from the king.

The noble thought he knew the problem. 'Perhaps he's too short of it,' he suggested. 'Don't you have a good slave for his bed?'

Cutha considered dubiously. Being deprived of sex did not usually make a man quite like this. He simply whistled up a female from somewhere, drew a couple of hours of enjoyment, and that was that. No, he mused. This was something that ran deep and it hit him—his tough brother was afraid.

This thought focused his attention on the situation in a more direct line. Now that he came to think about it, where was Calthus? The more he pondered and weighed up his brother's state of mind, the more it dawned upon him that something momentous was about to happen. Cutha could be brilliant but only at times. When he had odd flashes, they usually struck home with uncanny accuracy. He knew why Cenberht and Crida had ridden away on the king's errand—he had been present at the planning—but there was something else. What?

Cutha strolled over to his brother. 'Expecting Cenberht back?'

Ceawlin's mind was rotating in another direction. Cutha had started to think. He would ask this at the wrong time. 'Clear off, I wish to be alone!'

'We are brothers!' he pointed out mildly.

'So?' Ceawlin challenged.

'Thought it was time I reminded you!'

'Back off!'

Suddenly, there was a cry of warning from two of the sentries and a distant rumble of fast-moving hooves. A scout galloped into the tun, oblivious to passers-by. He pulled up with a violent swirl of hooves and dust.

'I've been sent on ahead. A patrol has

picked up three riders who were heading this way, and their mounts are nearly blown but no one has been hurt, and they are not pursued!'

Ceawlin jumped to his feet and Cutha was astounded to see his tough brother go pale. 'You are sure everyone is all right, the riders, I mean?'

The scout nodded. He had ridden at a manic pace, but knew the others would not be all that far behind. 'Yes sir! Three men, all sound of wind and limb, coming as fast as they can. But their mounts are very tired. They are also exhausted, and look as if they need a good feed.'

'Splendid!' Ceawlin bellowed as a great beaming smile broke over his face. 'Get food and drink organised now, now, I say!'

Cutha was astounded. Obviously Cenberht and Crida but who was the third man? Did they have a Briton as hostage? He knew he had a devious brother, and now their eyes met and Cutha saw the bad temper had vanished.

'It's worked! I've done it!' Ceawlin gloated.

'Done what?' Cutha shot back with exasperation.

Ceawlin threw back his head and laughed his pleasure. 'When these men have been fed I'll call a council meeting this afternoon, attend, and you'll find out everything. And I would strongly advise you to leave that woman and her stew-pot alone. The third man is her husband, and he could eat you up with one hand behind his back!'

The patrol came into view, with the three men tucked inside for absolute protection. The horses hung their heads with fatigue, their coats foam-flecked. They had been ridden long and hard and their riders slumped wearily. They halted before the king, dismounting very heavily, and lurched forward together in line abreast. Each man bowed his head, then looked up to his king. Calthus beamed from ear to ear. Cenberht's smile was that of a smug cat, while even Crida allowed his lips to twitch in the resemblance of a smile.

Ceawlin stepped forward and stopped before Calthus. 'Welcome back, senior earldorman!' he praised in a loud voice, so that all could hear. 'Now go to your good wife, but I will hold a council this afternoon.'

Calthus's chest swelled with pride. Now to find his darling Ethel. He marched off in a straight line and saw no one.

Ceawlin turned to Crida. 'There is a gift of gold for you!'

He turned to Cenberht . . . 'And I have something very fine and special arranged for you, my son. You will have a splendid wedding. The girl is very agreeable, and her father is now delighted. I will see that you and your bride will want for nothing!'

Cenberht's heart sank but he knew better than to say anything right now. It would have to wait until much later and his heart sank at the knowledge of the coming storm. A vision of Bracha's face floated into his mind and his resolve hardened. Come what may, she and she alone would be his wife.

They sat on stools well fortified with ale, and Ceawlin looked around with smug satisfaction at what was going to be a vital meeting.

'Calthus—give!' he demanded.

Calthus began to speak slowly, marshalling his thoughts into a coherent sequence of details and events. He was listened to in absolute silence until Cutha broke this with sheer amazement.

'I never thought to hear such words! Three British kings united against us? That certainly alters the balance of power!'

Ceawlin was also stunned. This put a different perspective on his battle plans. He was amazed how this had been managed so Calthus explained about a glib, rather smooth-talking, determined chief called Ralf.

'It was he who bought me from the Romanos, and he and his wife were decent slave owners, though I suspect that behind that persuasive tongue, Chief Ralf might just have a violent temper. He has a daughter, Bracha, whom I couldn't stand initially but when the chief was away, visiting these other kings, she took over and did quite a good job,' and Calthus paused to look fixedly at Cenberht.

Cenberht felt himself flush and lowered his

gaze. How much did Calthus know or guess? He squirmed uneasily on his stool and looked down to study the fresh reeds on the floor.

Ceawlin did not miss this and a tiny frown crossed his forehead in puzzlement. He opened his mouth to comment, then changed what he had planned to say. He would talk to the boy when all this was over, and they were alone.

Calthus continued. 'We Saxons are well and truly hated. The Britons have a slavish devotion to their land, and we are nothing but crafty, greedy invaders. I suppose in a way, they have a point, and it is my opinion that the Britons' antagonistic feeling has driven them into this very rare unification.'

'What about manpower?' the king asked.

Calthus pulled a face. 'It was not possible for me to find out the exact number of fighters who will oppose us but I have a nasty feeling it will be considerable. To hazard a guess, I would say, we might even be outnumbered three to one against. The king from Cirencester will bring a huge hoard with him and these fighters, combined with those from the other two kings, will make a formidable number,' he warned.

Ceawlin pulled a face at this distasteful information, which was completely unexpected. 'But what is their standard of fighting? Were you able to form an estimate? What about their food provisions and horses?'

Calthus gave him a steady stare. 'They will all fight to the death, because they're pretty good with their weapons, from what I saw when they practised. They also have this natural, almost colossal, drive to do away with an invader. Personally, I think this goes back to the Romans' 400 years of occupation. Their resentment at this has been so bitter that the very thought of a repeat experience is something for which they will gladly die. And die they will, and so will many Saxons! Do not, sir, underestimate these people. They have got stocks of food, they have excellent horses and are fairly well organised. They are not going to be any easy pushover!'

'Is that so?' Ceawlin drawled, but more to himself than the rest of them in general. 'What about communications?'

'There are many old tracks all over the place, plus the old Roman roads. These latter have not been attended to in decades, but they are still very capable of transporting fighting men from here to there,' Calthus explained.

'I wonder where they will meet us?' Ceawlin said slowly.

Calthus brightened. 'Oh! I can tell you that! They have picked a place called Deorham, and from what I overheard they will build defensive fortifications at the front.'

'But what about their rear?' Cutha asked with great interest.

Calthus turned to him. 'The place they have

chosen is on top of a fairly steep hill. And, I gather, they will ride to the battle site, leave their horses at the bottom and at the top of the hill fight on foot. Safe behind defensive barriers, which will be erected in time.'

'Is that so?' and a look crossed the king's face which was a mixture of amusement, and very smug satisfaction.

The others all looked at him expectantly, waiting for him to explain, but he declined. They looked at each other quite baffled and more than a little alarmed at the information they had been given to digest. To them what had started out as planning for a simple pushover fight had turned into something gravely serious. What had they all missed? The king knew something, but, rack their brains as they might, they could not work this one out. So they all turned and stared hard at their king and awaited his explanation with bated breath.

Ceawlin did not rise to this. It was not that he was being awkward or that he even distrusted his close advisers and companions. It was just sheer prudence, plus the fact he wished to mull over all this information when he was quite alone. He was so experienced in battle that years ago he had learned it was prudent to examine all possible permutations to avoid nasty, unexpected shocks.

Cutha was thoroughly disconcerted. All the fun and bounce had been knocked out of him. He also felt more than a little guilty at the realisation he had been hanging around a woman whose man had been brave enough to put his life on the line in such a horrible position. While he had been lolling through the last few months, doing his best to play foot-loose and fancy-free, Calthus had undergone humiliating hell.

Cenberht had listened, utterly appalled at this report. He was totally unimpressed with the Britons' plans, because he knew the king would have some superior advantage that he was keeping to himself. Thrash his brains as he might, he could not figure out what this could possibly be. What he did realise though was that his beloved Bracha could well be in the most appalling peril in the very near future. So where did that leave him? He was a Saxon through and through, and Bracha came from proven enemy stock, and his heart lurched and pained. He was very confident of his own feelings, which he knew would never change. And he also knew her feelings reciprocated his. So where did that leave them both?

Ceawlin kept throwing a look at this difficult son. What was wrong with him now? He was spending just a little too much time studying the floor rushes instead of displaying enthusiasm! There was something wrong somewhere and the king had a very nasty feeling he was not going to like whatever this was when he discovered it.

'There is one thing,' Calthus began, and his

voice became hard and bitter. 'There is a man there, a red devil, and I want him as mine. He goaded and taunted me at every available opportunity. I want to take him out personally!'

Crida frowned at this. 'I understand your feelings,' he began carefully, 'but I had quite a few jibes flung at me by that big redhead devil. I itched to take him on there and then, but—' and his words tailed off as he nodded towards Cenberht.

Calthus snorted. 'Like hell!' he rasped. 'You had just two days there. I had months of it! My claim is stronger than yours. I owe that vicious pig a lot!'

Crida stood abruptly, tipping his stool. 'I spoke first—he's mine!'

'Right is on my side, not yours!' Calthus snarled, also leaping to his feet.

Ceawlin realised he had to stop this otherwise these two would be at each other's throats. 'Shut up!' he bellowed in his best royal voice. 'I don't know the ins and outs of all this, but if you both feel so strongly about this Briton, gamble for him or, to keep the peace here, I'll take him out personally!'

Crida and Calthus whipped around in unison, horrified at the suggestion. 'No, sir, he's not your fight, he's mine!' they shouted together.

Ceawlin threw a questioning look at Cenberht who pulled a face and shrugged his shoulders. He was perfectly well aware that Melwas had riled Crida, but their time there had been so short. In his opinion Calthus certainly had the better claim.

'Gamble for him!' Cenberht agreed with the king.

Crida sulked a moment, then agreed. 'Very well,' he said reluctantly, determined to use his own loaded dice.

Calthus had the identical thought, and so did the king. 'We will use my dice!' he said pointedly. 'And that is an order. My decision will be final, because I will not have two of my men making fools of themselves over one Briton!' he shouted. Under other circumstances, this situation would have caused him vast amusement but today was not turning into one of his better days. What exactly was eating Cenberht?

He studied his son. How he had changed—it was amazing, and most discernible. Ceawlin wondered to himself. Had this been brought about by the nature of this successful enterprise? He could well imagine the stress under which Cenberht had operated. Yet how excellently he had performed his task. His heart swelled with pride, as well as a large stab of guilt. He reflected down the years, to his own callow youth. How like his late mother Cenberht looked, more so with each day that passed. She had been a lovely girl and he had genuinely wanted to marry her, but fate had arranged other plans for both of them. Now all was within his power as King as well as Father to reward with generosity.

Cenberht's own heart was now as tight as a new drum and filled with trepidation. He sensed what was coming, and he knew this was his personal trauma. He had re-examined himself and probed into the very depths of his heart and spirit, and knew he had not changed. He adored his Bracha and knew she, and she alone, was the other half of his spirit.

How crazy, though, it was going to sound when he aired these words. What made it worse was the fact she was a bitter enemy, by virtue of her tribe. Even those Britons who accepted the Saxons in the Thames Valley were not people whom the king regarded with much respect. The fact he could beat them in battle, made him look down his royal nose at times in a contradictory manner. He would hate Bracha automatically, just because she was a Briton.

What was she doing right now? What did she think of him, now he had run off with Calthus? She would have worked it all out and realised he was nothing but a glorified spy sent to extricate the man who had the vital information. She was incredibly bright, which was of the utmost importance to Cenberht. He did not want a female simply as a breeding machine. He wanted a companion who equalled him intellectually.

His heart quailed once more. He knew then that he was very much afraid of his father. It was not simply in his role as king, but also as a father with his well-known, awesome temper. He gulped noisily, and his heart hammered. Surely his father could hear it?

Ceawlin was deeply puzzled. Now why did Cenberht sit so mute with such a hang-dog look on his face? It was almost a sulk, which was ridiculous. He had performed a difficult task brilliantly so did he expect more lavish verbal praise? Surely not! That would be too effete. Yet they could not continue to sit like this. It suddenly hit him that perhaps Cenberht had a personal problem and had gone all shy on him. Was it because he was the king as well as a father? This idea put a fresh complexion on the situation.

Ceawlin cleared his throat. He had better give a little more praise before the reward. 'You did so well. I hardly know what to say to you,' he began carefully.

Cenberht lifted his head and blinked as if the words had not registered. Ceawlin was even more bewildered . . . If he did not want more praise what *exactly* did he want?

'Something bothering you, son?' he asked gently, coming in from a different angle.

Cenberht shook his head, then gave a miserable little nod. He felt the sweat break out on his forehead, and his breathing was too harsh and rapid.

'Don't worry,' Ceawlin said with forced cheerfulness, completely baffled with this attitude. 'I saw Eadgifu's father two days ago. I told him you were away but were expected back shortly. He is very happy now to agree to his daughter's betrothal to you. The other noble who was sniffing around for his son has backed off, though he's not very pleased at being pushed aside. That is his bad luck. As to the girl, you will meet her next week and you can both see what you think of each other. I promised her father there would be no pressure from either of us. But I think you'll be pleased. She's a pretty little thing and has good wide hips, so she should breed well for you.'

Cenberht became more appalled with each word from the king's lips. How the other noble must hate him and this was going to be nothing to what Eadgifu's father was going to feel. He took a deep breath, and his hand automatically went to his mother's lovely pendant before he remembered where it was.

Ceawlin did not miss the gesture, and he frowned. 'You are not wearing your mother's jewel!' he exclaimed. Had it been lost? That would be tragic! 'I can usually see the outline under your tunic!'

Slowly Cenberht stood in sheepish fashion, but head held proudly to face the storm. Ceawlin found himself copying but why did his own kingly heart increases its pace? There was

125

something very wrong somewhere. What in hell was his son going to come out with?

'It is with my betrothed,' Cenberht managed to get out at last and waited, holding his breath.

Ceawlin stared at him; for a few seconds the words did not register. He blinked, tilted his head to one side and decided he must have misheard.

'Say again!' he requested softly.

Cenberht knew perfectly well he had heard. 'Don't play-act now, Father! It is with the only girl I will marry. We are both betrothed. She is a Briton. She is the enemy!'

There, he had done it. Now would come the whirlwind.

NINE

Mona walked onwards thinking deeply, then her steps slowed and she halted Every nerve in her body twanged so she closed her eyes and let her instincts have full rein. She was still near to where she had stayed but, as always, she felt reluctant to back-track. Why then was something urging her to do just this?

Slowly she lowered herself to sit. She could not, dare not continue feeling like this, which was strangely unnerving for her. A new experience. Long ago, she had learned it was

126

extremely foolish to ignore her instincts and right now they were jabbing at her like spear thrusts.

She reviewed the general situation. A violent war was on its way, and she knew that others of her kind would also have picked up her own reasoning. No direct word will be spread around, but all the famous healing women would gradually start to meander down to the area where their skills would be vital.

A word here, another there, vibrations in the air from human emotion, would all total to make a scenario that screamed for help. Warriors on all sides never stood in the way of the healers because it might be they who needed their assistance next. It was true. There were many battle injuries that might require the healers' skills and instant death was always better than a lingering one. There were drugs which, when infused in a hot drink, released the suffering warrior's misery. Of all the possible battle wounds, none were more dreaded than the stinking disease for which death was the only cure.

Mona had long debated this condition with others of her ilk. Exactly how or why it occurred was beyond them. What was known was that an open wound that let in certain types of dirt was sure to rot the flesh. The wound would smell, turn black, give excruciating pain and have a disgusting, feral odour.

Human emotions could be equally tricky to heal, and never more so than when love reared its young head. Reason would vanish into thin air. The most staid, responsible person could become outrageously impossible. Bracha was certainly in that category, and all of a sudden Mona felt dread for her. She continued with her duties but a spark had vanished. She moved automatically. Even her speech was listless, confined to mere basics, and in her eyes there was a cloud of worry. It was simple to work out why. What was Ralf going to say?

She felt pity for Elesa. She had watched her first ridiculous marriage, and then when she was able to marry her Ralf, Mona had awaited the pangs of jealousy. These had never come and, analysing herself, she realised that, deep down, she had known and accepted the futility of where her own heart lay. Instead, she had become a firm friend to Elesa and had watched with interest the growth of their one surviving child, Bracha.

Mona was an expert at recognising trouble before it actually came to hand, and she knew now she would return. There was also the matter of the girl Ygraine. Mona knew Ygraine yearned to follow the healing calling and the girl certainly had skills. Initially, she had refused to consider her as a pupil, because Ygraine was just a little too much of a loose-tongued gossip, sometimes with a rather flippant attitude to all that went on around her.

She had changed, which amazed Mona and impressed her. Now Ygraine's attitude focused upon the slave Hoel. When she saw them together, Mona saw this could be an unusual match with great possibilities except that one was freeborn and the other servile. She doubted the slave would ever have enough coins to buy his freedom even if Ygraine was prepared to wait patiently. The trouble was Ygraine wanted Hoel—now! It was the old story of the mating game again. It had apparently never entered Ygraine's head that Hoel might have his own ideas on matters. What young man could respect the girl who did the chasing?

She sighed . . . Then there was Ralf. Although he adored his family, he could be tempestuous, very quick to strike out if provoked. He was going to return to a hornet's nest, because even the elders fretted for him to come back. This had always irritated Mona. The elders were supposed to be self-sufficient, and to be quite competent at coping for themselves in an emergency. She suspected that either it was getting beyond them or they had just become bone idle.

She was hidden where she sat, blending into the trees and plants on a narrow animal trail that ran parallel to a much wider one. She opened her eyes, narrowing them as she heard horses' hooves approaching. Gently standing, taking care to disturb no foliage, she peered with interest, then pulled a face. It was Ralf with his escort. She studied him carefully. He was thin to the point of being haggard and sat slumped on his mount as if he had no energy left. His escort were little better which meant they had ridden long and far.

There were many times when she was clairvoyant regarding the future, and now as she studied Ralf she felt incredible sadness. Was this the man with whom she had once been so much in love? How long ago that was, how little she had known and understood. She marvelled and speculated at the near future, as she turned her steps to head back to the vill again.

She slipped past the sentry, tut-tutting to herself, for he never saw her. Then she peered through at the little group of people who had gathered around Ralf and his escort. To one side stood Hoel, and Mona studied him with fresh interest. He did not know it yet, none of them did but herself, but this young slave was to be a major player in a drama to come. How would he react? More to the point, how would Ygraine react when she learned?

Of all the players soon to be involved she had studied them with care, except for one. The Saxon stranger was the true enigma and now he had vanished, leaving Mona more than a little frustrated at failing to complete the picture in her mind.

She saw Bracha appear with Ygraine a pace behind. Bracha was white-faced and tense. Ygraine touched her arm, said something but her friend did not hear, either because of her own personal stress, or because she was totally disinterested. Then Elesa appeared, and with a glad cry of welcome ran to greet Ralf as he dismounted to hug her.

Melwas was the next to stride into the tableau, roughly pushing two slaves from his path in his usual bumptious, odious manner. Mona scowled. What evil he bore was apparent and she reflected. She could just remember him as a child, and, even then, he had been fond of throwing his extra weight about. She knew that one day someone was going to take him out, and it would certainly be no loss to these people.

Melwas listened with interest to what one of the escorts was saying, then suddenly felt eyes glued upon him. His aggression flared instantly, and he swung around ready to fight, but when he realised whose hard eyes glowered at him he hastily looked elsewhere. Melwas had boasted for years that the man who could frighten him had not been born, which was perfectly true. Mona was another matter entirely. He could not understand her. Her eyes would hold his unblinkingly, and he would always be the first to break eye contact. To Melwas, Mona was shrouded in mystery, with awesome, inexplicable powers, which, deep down, terrified the life out of him. That which could not be dealt with by a fist or sword was that to be avoided—so Melwas hastily walked away.

He was disturbed without quite knowing why. Deep thinking was utterly beyond his limited intellect, but he did possess a sharp instinct. This now kept giving him a knifing prod, which disconcerted his well-being and re-ignited his flaring temper constantly. What his instinct told him he did not yet know but he was aware there was a subtle difference in the atmosphere. This was connected with the chief's daughter, and the runaway Saxon. He loathed Bracha's guts with a heartiness that was barely concealed.

Melwas had no time for females. In his eyes they had been placed upon earth to give a warrior sex and to propagate the species. He had been married three times and each wife had soon divorced him because of his brutality. This did not bother him, except when he thought he was being made a figure of fun over his matrimonial disasters. There were always female slaves, when he wanted sex, and as long as he did not mark or mar them too much, nothing was ever said.

He walked down to the riding animals, his eyes on the new slave Hoel. Here was a delicious new target, a frail youth too scared to fight a leaf. He opened his mouth to bellow and bully when he became aware that the slave was not alone.

Ygraine appeared from behind a horse and looked him in the eyes with harshness and—a challenge? Melwas scowled, looked at her, turned and saw Mona still had her eyes on him, and he backed down, swearing heartily.

As he walked away Hoel turned to Ygraine. 'He doesn't like me! What have I done, please?'

Ygraine let out a snort. 'Nothing!' she rasped. 'That surly swine doesn't like anyone but himself. I hate him!' she grated.

Then Ygraine's eyes turned to study Hoel. He had changed in a short space of time. His cheeks were no longer gaunt and hollow and flesh was appearing on his limbs. He was very good-looking, and she felt her heart throb. If only she knew what he thought of her deep down? Surely there was some way to find out without her making the running? Hopefully, she turned large, helpless lambs' eyes on Hoel who, bending to examine a horse's tendons, was totally oblivious to her.

Ralf came in to view again, eyes everywhere, missing exactly nothing. It was all a big act, because he felt like death warmed up. He knew the time had come to make domestic decisions that he had put off for far too long.

When he had first noticed the pain deep in his guts he was uncertain. What he did know was that his condition had deteriorated. He had lost flesh on his body, and his stools showed blood. He had heard of this before and knew there was no cure, so, warrior-like and man-like, he had kept it all to himself. There had been times when, cuddled up to him, Elesa's hands had explored ribs, which stood out into stark relief instead of being covered with flesh. He had hastily made excuses that the constant riding and arguing had affected his appetite so he was eating less. Elesa was a disingenuous soul and believed every word he uttered but Ralf now knew he was unlikely to fool her for much longer.

That he was a dying man was something with which he had managed to come to terms. It had crossed his mind to consult Mona, but the close friendship between the healer and his wife had made him hesitate. So he had stayed his questions which, he suspected, would not anyhow provide a profitable solution. He had concentrated instead upon this coming war with the Saxons when the whole of their tribal life would be under dire threat. He looked forward to the war now, because he would rather die in battle than writhe his last few weeks in the agony of whatever was eating away his guts.

Elesa was comely and in a year's time it was reasonable to assume she would take another mate. His big mistake, he acknowledged, was not doing something about his daughter before now. Bracha should have been married long ago, with one at her breast and another on the way. Instead, he had had allowed her to roam free and wild, but now must come the reckoning. Before he died, she had to be settled so that, at the very least, she would be able to look after Elesa. During all his numerous, recent long-distance rides, he had eyed up the available single males and, although not plentiful, there were a few who would do very nicely: fine upstanding young warriors, healthy, fit and keen for a mate. He had been particularly impressed with two warriors from the Cirencester area, and now it was his intention to move matters along on those lines.

He agreed that Bracha could be both stubborn as well as volatile, yet the brief report from Alun had showed she had managed his home area very well in his absence, even taking into account some ridiculous, half-garbled story of two Saxons, who had stayed here for a couple of nights. It was quite obvious to Ralf what they had been doing. It was unfortunate they had decamped, just before his return. He was particularly annoyed to realise the slave he had bought was also another one of the enemy. That stuck in his throat. Ceawlin had made a fool of him and would now have a full-scale, detailed report of their strength. At least he mused, he knew nothing about the other kings and their warrior bands . . . Then there was the further irritation of this new young slave called Hoel and the fact he had been so championed by Ygraine.

He had hoped to come back to just a little bit of peace and quiet but instead he had walked into uproar. He felt eyes fixed on him, turned and saw Mona. He ducked his head politely, walked over, looked deeply into her eyes and raised his eyebrows questioningly.

Mona smiled back, feeling immense pity but with enough wisdom to avoid comment of any kind. Ralf realised Mona knew he was a doomed man. They had no need for speech, words could be so trite, and Ralf was perfectly well aware of the feelings Mona had once had for him. That the healer was such a good friend to Elesa, despite losing her one true love to her, had always amazed him, especially as Mona lacked all bitterness.

'You know, don't you?' he asked in a soft voice.

Mona's look was incredibly sad, but she said nothing for one simple reason. There was nothing that could be said.

'Look after Elesa for me, will you?' he asked and paused a moment. 'I intend to make arrangements to get my daughter married, very quickly, before war starts, so that when the time comes Elesa will have someone to turn to apart from you,' he explained.

Mona held her tongue. The inevitable was obvious. There was going to be the most almighty row in Ralf's home and it was for this her instinct had about-turned her steps.

Ralf was not irked at Mona's silence, although he was a little puzzled that she passed no comment and asked no question about his daughter's intended. Then he shrugged whimsically. Mona was her own law and would speak only when she was good and ready. He patted her shoulder, confidentially.

'It will all work out!' he assured her, then turned and walked heavily back to his home.

Mona also departed to the little guesthouse, brought out a stool and sat half in and half out of the doorway. She could see everything that was taking place. She could also hear everything that was about to happen.

Elesa was worried. She had never seen Ralf so drawn or so haggard, and she quietly cursed the Saxons and all this trouble they were causing. A nasty suspicion had entered her mind to wonder if he was ill as well. Praise be that Mona had returned temporarily. This itself was so unusual as to make comment, and there was an ugly cold stone in the pit of her stomach. Had Mona returned because she sensed or knew Ralf was ill? As soon as discreetly possible, she knew she must see her friend and get the truth, good or bad.

Ralf sank on his stool and looked around appreciatively at the familiar possessions and comfort of his home. It was for all this that he had ridden so far, worked and argued so persuasively . . . He felt an enormous glow of satisfaction at the success of the mission. The three united kings with their huge mass of warriors were more than enough to halt this upstart Saxon in his tracks.

'Where is our daughter?' he asked a little gruffly as a pain knifed through his guts. 'I have to speak to her right now. Her marriage is long overdue, and I have met a couple of fine warriors for her to study. I want her to make arrangements to take an escort and ride to meet them. I want to see her wed before the war starts.'

Elesa stood still, quite thunderstruck. She could see that Ralf was in one of his very tetchy moods, and it would need very little for this to turn into a full-blown explosion. Then it hit her! It was for this reason that her friend had returned. She gave a little gulp, and stood frozen. What on earth was Ralf going to say?

'Wife, are you daydreaming, or do you know something I don't know? And that this something is not going to please me?' Ralf grated.

Elesa was bereft of speech by now when Bracha suddenly entered. Ralf spun on his stool and studied his daughter. She had changed while he had been away and not for the better either. Her face wore a bleak expression. It was white and drawn; why wasn't she looking him straight in the eyes, as usual?

'All right! What exactly has been going on here, while I was away?' he barked.

Elesa and Bracha exchanged uneasy looks, neither quite knowing what to say at that moment.

Ralf swore. He felt quite dreadful, and he was more than a little disconcerted at something that he saw pass between mother and daughter, and from which he was totally excluded. His senses and instinct jabbed a savage warning. 'Well? How many times do I have to ask?' he snapped sarcastically.

Bracha knew this was it. She turned to face her father, and look him straight in the eyes. 'I have become betrothed!' she said, shortly.

Ralf blinked with downright astonishment, while his mind raced over the available local warriors. 'Well?' he almost shouted.

Bracha took a deep breath and a grasp upon her personal courage. 'I have become betrothed to the Saxon Cenberht who stayed here a couple of nights!' There! It was out in the open at last. Now would come the storm and she gritted her teeth.

For five seconds Ralf was silent, totally speechless, then his mind moved into action with a bellow of rage. 'You are what? With an enemy spy? After only two days here? You have obviously gone stark raving mad, and I certainly will not allow such claptrap!' he shouted, furious with her, highly displeased with his beloved Elesa, who might at least have warned him and nearly doubling over with a fresh stab of pain.

Elesa stepped forward and held his left arm. With a violent shake, he pushed her away and glowered. She had known and not warned him, his temper elevated higher.

'Ralf,' Elesa protested. 'Control yourself You'll have a fit!'

Bracha stepped between them. 'It's all right, Mother, I can fight my own battles!' she told Elesa gently and shooed her outside. Then she faced her father, feeling sudden new strength flood her veins. 'I am adult, Father!' she started off quietly. 'I pick my own man!'

'Oh no you don't!' Ralf bellowed, nearly beside himself now. 'I am the chief. I am your father . . . I approve or disapprove, no matter how old you are. You stupid girl! Taken in by some smooth-talking boy still wet behind the ears and the enemy to boot! Even that Calthus went with him I've heard . . . another spy here all that time!' he ranted.

'Well, that's not my fault. I didn't know and anyhow, I didn't buy him!' Bracha shot back in her defence. 'You bought him!' she accused hotly.

Ralf's lips set in a tight line at this home truth. 'Pledging yourself to anyone after a mere two days! You want incarcerating for insanity!' He paused for breath. 'You'll forget this crass stupidity forthwith. Now get to your cubicle and there you stay until I say you can come out. I come back from hellish rides and meetings—to this!' he shouted. 'I never want to hear another word of your insanity again!'

Bracha gritted her teeth. 'We each pledged ourselves to the other because we fell in love as soon as we saw each other. It was like a lightning stroke,' she tried to explain desperately.

She sensed something dangerous in her father. She had never seen him like this before but she took a deep breath and held her ground. After all, she was his flesh and blood. How could he expect her to back down easily?

'I marry only him after the war,' she ended uneasily. That was her next awful fear.

'I'll see him dead first!' Ralf roared. 'Now get out of my sight!'

Bracha nearly obeyed, then changed her mind. She must, she simply had to try and make him understand . . . What was wrong with him? He was almost violent in his fury. 'I will marry only him!' she stated in a low but firm tone. 'And he will have only me!' she ended defiantly.

Ralf went berserk. He let fly with his right hand and it smashed against Bracha's left cheek and rocked her back on her heels. Not content with this, boiling with anger at her defiance, he backhanded her three more times. Then for good measure, he balled his fist and aimed at her unprotected jaw. Bracha went flying backwards, tripped over a small stool, and crashed down, temporarily winded.

Ralf halted then, aghast at what he had

done, half inclined to bend down and lift his daughter to her feet. He had no chance. With the resilience and speed of youth, Bracha scrambled to her feet, swayed for a few seconds, then acted with natural instinct. All she was doing was following the fighting training instilled in her by the man who had taught and trained her. Her father.

She snatched out her dagger and, holding it in the correct underarm position, with teeth bared in pain and humiliation, she lunged and for a heartbeat she meant it.

This fast move shook Ralf at the very second Elesa returned with Mona in tow. 'Stop it! Both of you!' Elesa screamed with horror. Even Mona was shaken, never expecting quite this.

The two protagonists froze as much from shock at the others' entry as at their own lethal intentions. Elesa jumped forward and chopped at Bracha's knife arm, hitting the elbow, making the weapon drop on the reeds. Then she spun around, and, with her face scarlet with fury and horror, slapped Ralf across his face, then stood in front of him and dared him to move, sparks flying from her eyes.

Mona was totally horrified. It was obvious there would be an explosion once Ralf learned about the Saxon, but even she had not been prepared for actions endowed with such lethal intent. Already Bracha's jaw had started to swell and turn a bright red. She was not very steady on her feet, keeping upright only by enormous willpower. Her head was a ball of thundering pain and internally she quivered with humiliation.

Ralf was still, flat-footed, knees bent, body perfectly balanced, eyes wide with shock at his wife's unexpected blow and the hard challenging look in her eyes. He felt a wave of shame course through him and averted his gaze. He flashed a look of hopeless appeal to the healer, then almost cringed physically at the cold implacable look in Mona's eyes.

He felt he had lost total control of the situation in general when his chauvinistic pride reared its ugly head. 'I am the chief here!' he almost snarled. 'I say what goes on here. I say who marries whom. Even the elders pay attention to me and I will *not* have this pigheaded girl daring to make decisions which will affect her whole life especially with an enemy spy after knowing him for just a few hours!' he bellowed, working himself into a fresh paroxysm of rage.

Elesa opened her mouth to try a diplomatic argument, then caught the tiny shake from Mona's head. She clenched her lips, balled her fists and stamped one foot on the reeds in her own anger and shock at this unexpected and horrific situation.

Ralf felt another stab of pain in his guts, but forced himself to stand erect and ignore it. 'You, girl, will go to your cubicle and stay there without food or drink until I say otherwise or until you regain your senses and agree to obey my orders and meet these two fine young men. If you don't, I will not hesitate to demote you to the status of slave—under Melwas!'

With a glare of triumph he saw his daughter flinch with horror. It was not just the thought of slavery, even as a temporary status, which cut her to the quick, but the knowledge that it would be under someone who despised her and for whom she had equal loathing.

'Now move or I'll throw you in your cubicle!' and he advanced a menacing step.

Bracha had enough sense to know when she was beaten. She spun on her toes and, crying with pain, shame and terrible humiliation, she fled to the little sanctuary of her cubicle to collapse on her bed and cry bitterly.

Ralf half-turned, gave a glare to Elesa, another to Mona, then stormed outside. He must be alone, away from everyone, to battle his pain, and his personal distress and disappointment.

Elesa stood flat-footed. Her instinct was to go to her daughter, and she moved half a step, but Mona gave a tiny shake of her head.

'Leave her be!' she advised in a soft voice.

Elesa felt the tears stream down her cheeks, and she lifted both hands helplessly. 'In all the years we have been married I never thought I would see Ralf behave like that!'

Mona hesitated a few seconds, while she

swiftly debated the appropriate words as she stepped forward, and rested one hand on her friend's shoulder. 'He is a sick man, you must bear with him,' she tried to placate.

Elesa struggled to control her tears. 'Well, don't just stand there, Mona! Do something!' she half-wailed.

Mona took a deep breath of frustration. Her heart filled with sorrow at what was to come in the near future and Elesa's blindness. 'There is nothing anyone can do for him,' she warned. 'He is not long for this life!'

Elesa's eyes opened wide, with fresh shock, and her jaw dropped, while her brow furrowed with anguish. Her mind worked with speed, as it ticked off points: Ralf's loss of flesh, his constant and unusual fatigue; this explosion of temper, extra violent even for one of his naturally, volatile nature; plus the terrible beating he had just administered to the daughter whom he, deep down, adored.

'You mean—?' she stammered, desperately wanting Mona to contradict her. As Mona stayed silent, Elesa's heart sank as her mind grappled with spears of fear coming from all directions. Finally she took a deep breath and managed to regain emotional control. 'What is going to happen then? What will he do?'

Mona took immense pity on her. 'He will do what any man in his position would do—with war coming!'

At last Elesa understood. 'He will let

himself die in battle!' and her head bowed with the enormity of what she had just admitted. It was so unfair and tears filled her eyes. 'I must go to Bracha and explain,' she began, but once more Mona shook her head firmly.

'Leave her for the time being with her hurt and humiliation but, under the circumstances, I think there is something you could do, and without any delay!'

Bending her head forward in a conspiratorial manner Mona began to speak rapidly. Elesa listened intently, giving a little nod now and again. When Mona paused, head slightly cocked to one side questioningly, Elesa slowly nodded. It all made sense now that she had the full facts but who was the best person?

'Who?' she wanted to know.

Mona gave one of her slow, secretive smiles and told her. Elesa's eyes opened wide with surprise but as she turned this information over she realised that, yet again, Mona was correct. 'Do you think he will? Do you think he *can*?' she asked, after a short pause for reflection.

Mona did not bother to reply. She had said her piece. She had interrupted her journey to come back, but now was the time to move on. She would have work elsewhere in the very near future, and quite suddenly, she itched to be on the move once more.

Elesa sensed this and hugged her old friend. 'Thank you,' she whispered. 'I will be all right now, I'm over the shock. I will do exactly as you say. May the spirits bless you, Mona!'

*   *   *

Bracha sat on her truckle bed, her mind still reeling with the shock of her experience. The physical pain was bad enough, but much worse was the knowledge that her once beloved father could turn into a brute to try and crush her spirit. In her life to date, he had never once hit her, so the thrashing she had just received was something she could hardly understand.

Her jaw set in a grim line. She was not her father's daughter for nothing. She would not see these two warriors. She would not be a slave to that odious Melwas. She would have to flee but where and how and what about her mother? Questions hammered at her as her fingers touched the pendant. She felt the warmth of the jewel, and a light smile touched her as she pictured Cenberht's face. Upon reflection, their betrothal after just a handful of hours was insane, but not enough to warrant the beating or the slavery threat. She struggled to force her mind to act logically, but she was still too confused and too hurt.

Her door opened suddenly, and her mother appeared with a bowl of cold water and a soft animal skin. Without a word, Elesa sat nearby and started dabbing the cold water on the rapidly swelling bruises.

Elesa had debated with herself how much to relate to Bracha and finally decided not to say a word about Ralf, if possible. Current practicalities were far more important now.

'Now pay attention, girl, and listen to me. I don't want to repeat myself twice. I want you to take all this in before your father returns!' and she began to speak rapidly in a low voice, outlining Mona's brilliant idea.

Bracha sat frozen, then as the import of the words sank in, her spirit began to rise a little. So there was a chance for her, after all, to get away from here, and to find Cenberht.

'Now have you taken it all in?' Elesa asked anxiously. 'We know the battle is going to take place at Deorham, and I seem to remember there are a couple of hills there. You will go there and wait, but you can't go alone. That I won't have. The best person to be with you is Ygraine. I'll see you take plenty of food because you will have to cold camp. It's unlikely you will be able to light a fire unless you can find a very sheltered spot in a dip and even then you must burn only very dry wood so there will be no smoke to give away your presence. Not only will you be hiding from our people but also from the Saxons, and you can be sure they will have scouts out as well.'

'But Cenberht—he won't know I'm there!' Bracha protested with a little rush of words.

'Oh yes, he will, because—' and lowering

her voice almost to a whisper just in case a slave was eavesdropping, '—I am going to send Hoel to find him, explain exactly where you are, and what has happened, so that he can come and join you!'

Bracha gasped as fresh hope filled her completely. 'But will he do it?'

Elesa nodded feverishly. 'He will, because I have the best bait in the world. Manumission! [Manumission is the act of freeing a slave, done at the will of the owner.] I will write a paper giving him his freedom, stating he is a free man on a special exercise for me and to be given all the help imaginable!'

Now Bracha understood. 'And that is why you want Ygraine with me!' and she marvelled at the beauty of the plan. 'It's brilliant, Mother!'

'Don't thank me, thank Mona when next you see her!'

'And Father with you?'

'Don't you go worrying your head about him. I can handle him!' she lied with a smoothness that astonished her when she knew her heart was breaking in two. 'Now let's get down to details. I'll see your father has plenty to drink tonight, so you slip away. Just before dawn. I'll speak to Ygraine and I'll frighten her to keep a still tongue in her head for once. I have a hold on her and she's going to find out very quickly. If she can keep her mouth shut and do exactly as I say, Mona will

149

take her on as an acolyte. Let her put one toenail wrong, and she will be finished for the rest of her life. You are to take two decent horses and I'll give you some pelts so that you can call in at the Romano traders. Change horses there and leave a sealed message for your Saxon. I will see that Hoel understands everything and I will even draw him a sketch map. I think he is a very bright young man, and to become a free man will be the height of his ambition. There is one thing, though, Melwas will be taking his turn at sentry duty and I don't know exactly where. The elders have been changing them around a bit, so you will have to be very careful when you do finally leave!' she warned in a sober voice.

Bracha nodded seriously. 'Is it wise to go to the Romanos? I don't think they like us very much,' she explained soberly.

'It is the best place to leave a message for your Saxon to collect!' she told her. 'I will even draw a rough sketch for Hoel to carry with him so no mistake is made. While I go and see where your father is, and attend to his mood, you keep bathing your face, and then get some rest. When you father comes back in, stay here. Do not come out. It will only antagonise him again. Let me get him drunk first!' and she could have screamed with the pain in her own heart, but with a mighty effort of will she kept her expression bland.

TEN

It was rare, almost unheard of, for King Ceawlin to be totally lost for words. He stood, frowning heavily, trying to understand Cenberht's words. What exactly had he said? He was already betrothed? And to a—Briton? His frown changed to an ugly scowl while his jaw set pugnaciously. The precious jewel pendant had been given to one of the enemy? His eyes narrowed and he bent his head forward and still towered over his son. For a Saxon he was exceptionally tall and though Cenberht could never be classed as small, he looked almost puny against his mighty sire.

'Repeat that!' Ceawlin growled.

Cenberht shook his head. 'No, Father. You heard me perfectly well the first time!'

'But you were only there a few hours!' Ceawlin grated, still more bemused than livid.

Cenberht threw him one of his dreamy smiles. 'That's true, but it was an instant thing for both of us. And I have heard that true love can strike like this, but I never thought it would happen to me!' he marvelled as tenderness swept over his face. 'She felt exactly the same too!' he added before continuing, 'I know it sounds crazy. We both thought that as well. Yet we are so sure. She is the most wonderful girl I have met or will ever meet. She is perfect in all ways, looks, spirit, figure but, above all, in intellect,' he beamed happily, once more reliving it all. 'She is well bred too, a chief's daughter, and wears a lovely golden torque.'

Ceawlin had been thrown many puzzles in his life, and he had also experienced more than his fair share of shocks but this information pole-axed him temporarily. If anyone else had spoken like this he would have branded them insane on the spot. With this peculiar and highly unusual son—of whom he was now so proud—the information was like a double slap in the face. Then the full implications struck home.

'Betrothed? Without my consent? A king's son! I'll not have it!' he roared. 'I will say whom you will and won't marry! I've gone to enormous trouble to arrange a splendid match for you, which happened to cost me quite a bit in bribes and hush money. I told you someone else wanted the girl, but after much hard talking and even more difficult haggling, her father has agreed to save her for you only. Apart from anything else, I should look an absolute idiot before everyone!'

Cenberht gave the king his full attention and pulled himself back from a lovely daydream. 'I am of age, Father,' he pointed out coolly. 'And I didn't ask you to go around arranging my life for me. After all, for years you have ignored me, because I was base born, which I might add, was not my fault!'

Ceawlin cringed a little at this and opened his mouth to pursue one particular line of argument but Cenberht forestalled this.

'What do you think it's been like for me all these years?' he asked with a sudden coldness. 'How do you think I've felt being mocked at and jeered from a small boy upwards. You weren't sufficiently interested in me to come down on my side then, were you, Father? I was just ignored year in year out by you, the king, my sire!'

Ceawlin was shocked, and at the same time, filled with guilty unease at the truth of these hard-hitting words.

Cenberht was now well away as years of bitterness finally came into the open. 'How do you think I felt at the snide remarks made about my poor mother who died to give me life. What did you care? What did you do? Nothing at all!' he accused hotly. 'But when you want something special done I become good enough. You rediscover me. I am useful! Now you have the nerve to tell me whom I may or may not marry. Well that won't do in my eyes. If I wasn't good enough to you before, Father, then I'm not good enough now for you to quibble over she whom I have chosen as my future mate. I repeat—*whom I have chosen!*' and Cenberht realised he was shouting.

Ceawlin stood quite astounded at this

totally unexpected display of wrath. Who would've thought the boy had this in him? He had always seemed such an ineffectual dreamer, yet behind all that there was fire and steel. He felt his heart swell again with fresh pride but he knew what his next action must be. Defiance could only be allowed to go so far. He and he alone was the dominant male, the king of all the Saxons and everyone must bow their head to him or go under. One slight sign of weakness, and he would lose total control, and even possibly be usurped from his position. He was—the king!

'Why you miserable whelp! I go to all that trouble, I bend over backwards, sweet talking the girl's father around, I give a delicate heave to another noble's aspirations and you stand there and tell me it's none of your doing? Of course it is! It's all your fault from start to finish! You have spent too much time blowing around the slave girls and, anyhow, you are long overdue for marriage. It's indecent that someone of your age isn't already married with a child at foot! I'll not hear anymore of this rubbish of yours. I'll thrash these Britons and put *her* into slavery, where she obviously belongs!'

'Over my dead body!' Cenberht grated and now he changed. 'She is mine, all mine! You harm one hair on her head and, king or no king, I'll kill you. There is one thing you had better remember, Father. I am your son, and like follows like!'

Ceawlin jumped forward and smashed one fist into Cenberht's jaw The younger man crashed backwards, lay a few seconds, stunned with shock, while the king looked down at him, a smile on his face. Cenberht rubbed his jaw, then slowly stood but suddenly he was no longer the dreamy youth his father knew. Neither did he resemble any more his long dead mother. He was a stranger who boiled with rage.

'Don't threaten me, puppy, until you have proved yourself in battle!!' Ceawlin raged at him then drew his fist back again, blood lust apparent.

Cenberht knew he had no chance at all in a fist fight, because he lacked his father's height, weight and strength. On the other hand, he came from this man's same bloodline, and he had his own temper when it was finally ignited. He exploded.

He jumped forward and let drive, hitting Ceawlin flush in the guts. As the king winced and half doubled, Cenberht slammed again and this time his blow landed on the king's cheekbone. Within seconds, both of them were going at it hammer and tongs, with the younger man getting the worse. The uproar they made carried outside.

Cutha opened the door, peeped in and froze, disbelieving his own eyes. 'What in Hades—?' he began, then his brother turned and snarled at him.

'Get out! This is a family matter!' Ceawlin bellowed, pausing to catch his breath while Cenberht sprawled, yet again, on the ground.

Cutha was stunned with shock. It was a long time since he had seen Ceawlin in such a fighting rage. He banged the door behind him, but held his ground. 'I do happen to *be* family!' he said mildly.

'Get out!' Ceawlin snarled once more.

'No I won't. I'm going to stay here to make sure murder is not committed!' Cutha said flatly, though keeping a wary eye on Ceawlin, in case he was the next intended target.

The room was a wreck. Furniture was broken, reeds had been dragged aside, two wall hangings had been ripped down and the din was appalling. Cutha was well aware that, outside, a number of people had gathered wondering with great interest who was murdering whom and why?

Finally, Cenberht knew he was beaten. He was just about thrashed senseless. Blood poured freely from his lips, which had begun to swell. In the morning he would have two huge black eyes, and his jaw felt fragile with pain. He lay slumped without an ounce of energy left. He tried to scramble to his feet, half made it, then slumped back down again, breathing heavily through a badly pummelled nose which also streamed blood.

Strangely enough Cutha noted, although his

brother did not have such a bloody mask of a face, he stood feet apart and swayed very gently. He also breathed very heavily, and there was a gap in his mouth where a precious tooth had departed.

It was obvious that, although very badly beaten, his nephew had given a good account of himself even though so much lighter in weight. Cutha's eyebrows elevated with interest. What it was all about, he had not the faintest idea, but serious it certainly was. He had not seen Ceawlin behave like this since a long-ago boyhood fight.

No one spoke. The fighters steadied their breathing and, gradually, with an enormous effort, Cenberht pulled himself to his feet and stood right before his father.

'I will not!' he repeated.

Ceawlin could hardly believe his ears at this repeated defiance. He snarled, drew back a fist again when Cutha caught his arm.

'Enough!' his brother said, almost placidly. 'I think it is better we save our fighting for the enemy, and not brawl among ourselves.'

His words registered and Ceawlin faced him. He was quite right, of course, and as the king he should have allowed discipline to be administered by another party. Deep down, though, he was simply amazed at the punishment his son had taken without a whimper, yet having the gall to continue to defy him! His heart flooded with tremendous pride, and it took an effort for this not to show on his face or in his eyes.

With his breathing steadying at last, Ceawlin turned to his brother. 'Take him away and lodge him with the oxen and use him as a pack oxen. He is not human until I say so again. When we march, he will be a beast of burden. He will only eat after everyone else, and then with the minimum food. Any trouble of any kind, and I personally will brand each cheek with a white-hot branding iron and it will be with the mark of the outlaw, and I will then expel him from all society!'

Cutha stood aghast and horrified. He could not remember when he had last heard such an horrific sentence. He snapped one look at the king's face and knew this was neither the time nor the place to ask any question whatsoever. He grabbed the younger man by his arm and led him outside, where his appearance provoked comments from a highly interested audience. Cutha waved one hand warningly, and they all carefully backed away, leaving him with the rather battered and sorry young man.

Carefully Cutha steered him to the end of the encampment, where the animals were kept. Cenberht could hardly hold himself up as he staggered and swayed with exhaustion and pain. There was a small pen with a little bit of straw in one corner and Cutha gently lowered him, then fetched a beaker and gave him some water.

'Well,' he began thoughtfully, 'you certainly don't do things by half measures!' Then something hit him. 'But what exactly *have* you done to take such a beating?'

Cenberht drank thirstily, then swilled the water around his mouth, while his tongue checked that he was lucky enough to still retain all his teeth, although two did feel very loose. He threw a peculiar, lopsided grin at the man bending over him.

'I have fallen in love with and become betrothed to a Briton I met during the few hours I was in her tun, Uncle!' His lips twisted into a painful grin with great effort. 'That's all!'

Cutha was staggered. 'That's all, he says!' shaking his head. 'And after only a few hours, a member of the enemy race, when your father's been at great pains to get you married into a noble Saxon family! You are lucky to be still alive and breathing!' he marvelled. 'Have you gone quite out of your mind?'

Cenberht managed a tiny shake of his head. 'You would understand, Uncle, if you had met her. She's the one and only for me, and the king can do what he likes, rant, rave and pummel me again but if I don't have her I stay single for the life that is left to me and that, by all the spirits, I vow!'

Cutha fell silent with amazement. Not in a hundred guesses would he have arrived at this deduction. By all the gods imaginable, what kind of girl was this enemy Briton? He knew now he would have to have a few quiet words with both Crida and Calthus. At present though his brother had to be obeyed to the letter. Ceawlin in his present mood was a highly dangerous man, who would not hesitate to kill anyone who dared to defy him further.

'Clean your face up a bit with this water,' and he fetched a pail with fresh water and some soft hay. 'You are going to feel like hell in a few hours time so take it easy. I'll come back later and try and bring you some rations!'

'The king?'

Cutha led out of snort. 'I'm used to him. Anyhow, although he's two years older than me I used to beat him when we were boys. I expect I could probably manage it now even though I have a bit of a midriff!' and Cutha patted his middle, where a line of fat did show .'Also, I could still outrun him, if push comes to shove. Don't you worry your head about me. I've dealt with Big Brother before in all his moods!!' and with an artificial smile, Cutha strolled away.

This was indeed a serious matter and he knew he had to talk to his brother but he would have to pick his time. When all was said and done, Ceawlin did have the power and majesty of being a king, while he, Cutha, was just the spare.

Cenberht knew he felt like death warmed up. He had never felt so exhausted in all his life but also, it was the first time he had ever been in a genuine fight. In the morning he knew he would be in agony and the thought that he was relegated to being but a pack animal stuck in his throat. What a stinking, lousy rotten mess, but then, he reminded himself, had he expected anything else?

What about Bracha? He bit his lip anxiously Would her family also be violently opposed? What if she had been made to suffer as well? A chill cascaded down his back and he was furious to feel tears prickling at the back of his eyes. He had not wept since a small boy and he would not do so now. Neither would he wallow in self-pity. He had gone into this with his eyes open, and he regretted nothing.

Bracha, his spirit cried to the sky. Where are you? What have they done to you? Because, suddenly, he knew she would not be unscathed either. There was do so much hatred between Britain and Saxon; both fathers would be vitriolic when they learned the truth.

He gritted his teeth. How could he leave her to suffer in her tun? But what could he do in his present condition? It would be days, perhaps even as long as a week, before he recovered enough to move more easily. Once this did happen he had to go and get her out and away from her people. The Britons would have no chance at all against his scheming, cunning father. Then an horrific thought entered his head. She was trained in all weapons so what if she were forced into the war to fight Saxons?

He ground his teeth together impotently. There was absolutely nothing he could do at the moment, or even in a few days' time. He could not expect too much help from his uncle, because that would be unfair. Crida he dismissed right away. Calthus? Out of the question. After nine months of slavery, he would itch to fight Britons and his shoulders slumped as he realised he was all alone, without one ally in the world.

He turned over the problem. He had to get away and see Bracha but surely it was better to wait a few more days. This would give him time to recover from the beating and if he was going to be a pack animal, following the king's army, he would be moving in the correct direction. Whether he could escape alone was problematical.

Deep down, he knew his father's threat of outlawry was not an idle one. It was not just the branding on each cheek with a white-hot iron but what could come afterwards. He had once seen a man branded an outlaw, and his body had been discovered days later. The wounds had turned foul, black and stinking, and some noxious poison had gone all through the man's body. He had died alone and in agony.

Anyone branded an outlaw, even if the wounds did heal clean, was assured of only a very short life. Man was a herd animal like a horse. In the vile winters, where could a lone man go for food, shelter and warmth? Man needed other men for physical and practical company. More to the horrific point, an outlaw was fair game for any man or woman or child to kill with complete impunity. No questions asked. No court. No nothing. It was a very frightening prospect, and even he quailed at the thought of being branded an outlaw.

This meant he was doomed to stay with the Saxon war band until he could even the odds or bring them down on his side, which meant he had to have a reliable ally. He did not.

The day waned, and when it was night Cutha appeared with a little food on a platter and some ale. He handed it over with a wry grin.

'If my brother knew I was doing this I will probably be joining you!' he quipped, though he looked around uneasily to make sure they were both unobserved.

Cenberht was grateful and knew he could not say a word about any plans he might manage to formulate to escape and save his beloved.

Cutha eyed him curiously. 'What you intend to do?' he asked gently.

Cenberht pulled a face and stayed silent. He looked long and hard in his uncle's face and realised Cutha understood the reason for his reticence. A smile twitched the older man's lips, and he nodded approvingly.

'When my brother gets in one of his tempers it is better he is left strictly alone and not crossed by anyone,' he agreed thoughtfully. 'He's just had another bad experience, which has pushed his temper up even higher. He has had to go and see the girl's father, call it all off, make his peace with him and then have a little chat with the other noble whose nose had been pushed out of joint. I do hope this British girl is worth all this uproar,' he added dryly.

Cenberht managed a grin though winced at the pain of his lips. 'She is! To me!'

'Well, the only advice I can give you is to try and get some strength back into your muscles and do nothing until you feel more like your old self. I shall have to work you tomorrow, to placate the king but that might not be a bad thing. It will all help to loosen you up and disperse the bruising. I think we should probably march to war sometime within the next one to two weeks. There will be no hurry, of course. It will be a leisurely march. We know where we're going. The Britons will be ready for us, so we can take our time in order to arrive very fresh in fighting fettle. You just concentrate on getting back your strength. If you see the king, no matter what you feel, do not antagonise him. It rebounds on the rest of us as well as you!' he added.

Cenberht understood. He felt grateful to his

uncle and wondered quietly why he hadn't bothered to get to know him before. He had made a lot of mistakes but then, he reminded himself, who doesn't if they are human?

*   *   *

Bracha knew she had never felt so dreadful in all her life. She had a vile headache while the rest of her face pounded and throbbed agonisingly. Worse than these physical miseries was the knowledge of exactly who had done this to her, and why. When she thought back she was forced to acknowledge Ralf had turned into a terrifying monster. A person who only lived in her worst nightmares. Where had the loving and doting father varnished? It was quite incredible to have to acknowledge that the one for whom she had always had the greatest respect and admiration was now relegated to being someone of the utmost loathing.

When her mother slipped quietly in with bulging saddlebags, it took an effort of will for her to stand and look at her miserably.

'Why? Why did he act like such a savage animal? Why, Mother!' she cried, but had sufficient presence of mind to keep her voice low.

Elesa sat down on the edge of the bed consumed with the utmost weariness and fear. Again and again, she had gone over her friend's words and, very slowly, she had begun to accept them. It seemed incredible that such a wondrous relationship was coming to what was going to be the most bloody awful end. And there was not a thing she could do about it. This was the hardest truth of all to accept and to keep to herself.

'One day I'll explain but this is neither the time nor the place. What we have to concentrate upon doing now is getting you right away. Your father is in a drunken stupor, but in the morning when he awakens he'll be as bad as half a dozen bears with sore heads.'

'Mother, I'm worried about leaving you here with him!' Bracha replied anxiously.

Elesa gave her a wan smile and patted one shoulder. 'I can look after myself, daughter!' and she took a deep breath. 'Now you must listen carefully to me and take in everything I say. Your whole future is going to depend upon the next few hours.'

Bracha took a deep breath and forced the headache aside so she could concentrate. 'Go on, Mother!'

'I have spoken with Hoel and, as suspected, he would cheerfully commit murder to become a free man. I have been frank with him and given him all the details of what has happened and why. I could do no less, because it is going to take considerable bravery to ride up to the Saxons and, somehow, get into their camp or marching band to find your young man. What

166

exactly will happen afterwards, I cannot imagine. We are going to leave everything to Hoel, because he will be the man on the spot.'

'Has he been thoroughly briefed?'

Elesa nodded. 'I am pretty certain he knows where to go to meet up with you in due course. But getting away with another person is going to be pretty tricky for him.'

Bracha nodded soberly and swallowed fretfully. How was her beloved Cenberht? Did he think of her often? Was she in his mind? And how was he? She had heard fearful stories of the king of the Saxons, who had the reputation for being a very hard man. How would this king react when he learned one of his men was betrothed to one of the enemy? The questions hammered at her mercilessly, so with enormous willpower she thrust them to the back of her mind.

Elesa continued quietly. 'I have also had a very long talk with Ygraine. I have made it very clear that if she even thinks of gossiping to anyone at all, she will have ruined her life for all time. In short, I have frightened the living daylights out of her. I think you'll find she is very sober and subdued when you meet up, and for your own survival keep her like that. It is obvious the three of you cannot just ride away from here. We must be more subtle!'

'How?' Bracha asked with bated breath. It was incredible that her quiet, gentle mother should turn into such an adroit schemer.

'The weather is quite good, so I have sent her and Hoel off in advance. I told them to take two horses from the small herd outside, to walk away and not to mount and ride for quite a distance. Remember that clump of trees where lightning split the oak? They will wait there for you!'

Bracha chewed this over in her mind. 'Those horses are not very good ones,' she pointed out. The very best ones had always been kept near to hand for emergency riding.

Elesa nodded. 'That's quite true, but you can go to the Romanos and trade up. I sorted out some good skins and pelts for barter. With these you will be able to mount yourselves properly, when the three of you are together. Then ride for where we agreed, but not in a direct line. Your father is going to explode again, and you can be sure he'll send trackers out after you. Use rough ground, ride up streams, cover your passage to the best of your ability.'

Bracha turned it all over in her mind then a twinkle appeared in her bruised eyes. 'The elders will think Hoel and Ygraine have stayed out overnight to have it off!'

This was a point which had not escaped her mother and she managed a little smile herself though it took an effort. 'Why not indeed! They are young with hot blood, though, I think Ygraine might be going to get rather a shock. When Hoel took it in that I had made him a

168

free man, by the power vested in me as the wife of a chief, he seemed to grow and swell with pride. Ygraine might just find that her sick, weak patient has changed to a dominant man!'

'Do her good!' Bracha snorted unsympathetically.

Elesa eyed her, and even felt a little amusement. Did not her daughter realise she too might make the same discovery in the very near future if their plans went to fruition? She forced her thoughts back down again on the sensible path of practicalities.

'There is one other point, which is not in our favour. After your father found out what had been going on here he went over to the elders and issued a lot of fresh instructions. All the sentries have been doubled, and they are going to be changed every couple of hours to make sure no one falls asleep. What this means is you are going to have to have a cast-iron excuse to ride away from here at the dawn because you will certainly be challenged. And out of this tun, you must certainly be before the sun comes up, and a thoroughly bad-tempered Ralf awakens!' she warned grimly.

This sobered Bracha. 'I was going to take one of the better horses, and—' then her words tailed off, and she looked anxiously at her mother.

Elesa considered. 'Still do that, because you're going on an errand!'

'Am I?'

'Yes! You are going after Mona! She had you pick some herbs for her, but accidentally left them behind. You are going to take them to her!' and Elesa dived into a tunic pocket and brought out some fronds of greenery. 'Here! You are taking these!'

Bracha eyed the plants dubiously. 'Are they herbs or healing plants?'

Elesa shrugged. 'I haven't the faintest idea. I picked them just before I came over here. They could be weeds as far as I know but I very much doubt that any of our sentries would know any better!'

'Mother—you are marvellous and priceless!'

Elesa knew her tears now threatened and she stood rather brusquely. 'Rest, I will come for you just before dawn. I do so hope your Saxon is worth all this.'

'Oh Mother, he is. If I don't have him as my man, I will have no one at all!'

To her surprise, after her mother had left, she dozed off and fell into a proper sleep. She awoke with a start with Elesa shaking her shoulder. All was quiet and dark, and she fumbled to dress. Her headache had gone with the resilience of youth but when she ran her fingers over her face, she realised it was swollen, puffy and tender.

Elesa watched her wearily. Once Bracha's departure was known, Ralf would explode again, and he would send out a search party.

Defiance he would not stand. She felt tension and increased stress at the situation in general, and her own heartbreak in particular. What was going to be the outcome for all of them? All they asked to do was live a quiet life with their own customs. This dreadful upheaval was the result of King Ceawlin and his avaricious greed for more and more of their land under total Saxon domination. He was every bit as bad as the Romans of old.

ELEVEN

Because Melwas had a low intellect, it took him a considerable time to arrive at any conclusion. In the process, his final deductions would always be black or white. The in-between greys never existed. Conversations were the same because he lacked the ability to read into a nuance. Facts and reasons had to be spelled out laboriously in bare simple statements.

When he did finally arrive at some decision, after many weary hours of mental tussle, he became rigidly inflexible. If he had been more of a sociable person, people would have taken the time and trouble to explain in detail but Melwas knew he was unloved to the point of being hated. So what, he never failed to ask himself, he could thrash nearly everyone around and it bolstered his peculiar and unnatural ego to see how most men moved from his path.

What he did have, though, was great animal cunning and a very unusual hobby. Because of his isolation he had always been in the habit of wandering into the wild, observing and noting. This gave him great skill as a hunter, which no one in the tun could fault. He was also highly observant, regarding foliage and plants in general. Although he was in awe and fear of the healer he had always made it a point to follow wherever she wandered at a very discreet distance at her rear.

Mona had always been perfectly well aware of this, and with a better-tempered person she would have gone out of her way to stop and explain what she picked and why. Melwas, she totally ignored, with odium. So in his way he had picked up an above average working knowledge of plants, which he had kept entirely to himself. It was this oddity which was to be Bracha and Elesa's undoing.

Bracha moved very silently, as she selected a horse. Two hounds came up to investigate this unusual activity in the dark but she let them take her scent, and after some interested snuffles the hounds wandered away to investigate elsewhere.

With her horse ready, she mounted quietly and nudged it into a slow walk to one of the tun's exits. She had no idea at all which sentry was on guard and where. Very slowly, faint streaks of light had appeared in the eastern sky and, as her eyes had also adjusted, she could see reasonably well.

It was all so quiet, with most sensible people still in bed. She felt an ache in her heart. She was leaving her home area, a place she had always known and relished since old enough to be aware of anything at all, and there was an ugly lump in her throat. Then a vivid picture of Cenberht flashed in her mind and she took a deep breath of reassurance. It was all going to work out. It had to!

Melwas heard the horse approach and frowned with suspicion. It had finally dawned upon him that there was something very wrong with this place. To start with, why hadn't he seen that cheeky girl Ygraine? And also where was that slave boy Hoel? Were those two out in the night by themselves? It would give him great pleasure to pass this information onto the elders. Then there was all that uproar yesterday, which had come from the chief's house. He itched to know what that was about. Another unusual event had been the reappearance of the healer when she had already left once. It was unheard of for Mona to put in a second visitation so soon after the first. His animal instinct told him there was a uniting thread to these peculiar events that at present he was quite unable to grasp.

But a horse plodding forward, just before

dawn, was another matter entirely. It was hostile. He waited until the sound approached even nearer, then stepped into view, spear held aggressively in his right hand.

Bracha jumped with shock then her heart sank. The sentry would have to be—him! Melwas too was temporarily stunned into silence. He gazed at the girl's battered, swollen face, and finally added this to the uproar he had heard the previous day from the chief's home. For a few seconds he was amazed, barely able to recognise the girl. What a beating she had taken and he nodded to himself in thorough approval of the chief's actions. What it was all about was immaterial to him. What the chief had now done was something that should have been dealt out long ago. This girl had always fancied herself and looked down her nose at him.

'Well, well!' he drawled and laughed wickedly. 'I see our chief's come to his senses at last and given you the thrashing you have long deserved.'

Bracha bit back a retort with an almighty effort. It was vital she get past him. Where strength and weight were concerned, the odds were now very much against her.

'Get out of my way!' she snapped.

'And just where do you think you are going at this hour?' Melwas snarled and stepped forward a pace.

Bracha struggled to regain her wits. 'I am

174

going after the healer!' she gabbled frantically. 'She left some other healing plants behind, and I'm taking them to her!'

Melwas gave her a very hard look. 'Is that so? Show me!' he shouted, his voice now reverberating everywhere.

Bracha frantically dived into her to tunic and thrust the rather crumpled green plants in Melwas's face while she prepared to heel her horse forward in a mad dash.

Melwas grabbed a rein and halted this ploy, while he looked disparagingly at the plants. 'Crap!' he snarled. 'Those are nothing but weeds. I've forgotten more about plants than you will ever know. You are lying in your teeth. The chief gave you a deserved beating and you think you're going to run away. Bolt to join up with the other two who are missing! Get off that horse. If you're going anywhere it's back to the chief right now!' he snarled with exultation. This would be a fine feather in his cap. People would look up to him at last!

Bracha knew she had a few heartbeats to act to save herself. She lifted up her left leg, drew it towards herself and kicked Melwas on the point of his nose. He let out a howl of anguish as Bracha rammed her heels into the horse's ribs. The startled animal shot into a jolting canter, then was past the sentry.

Melwas lurched to keep his balance as the horse's quarters swung into him and he roared again. Like a lot of big men though, he could, when provoked, move with surprising speed. He whipped around, darted to one side and grabbed the reins of his own horse, which had been kept nearby, unknown to anyone. With one vault, he was astride and chasing after her as blood streamed down from his nose.

Bracha's heart was in her mouth. Once clear of the tun, she heeled her horse into a hard gallop and prayed the animal would not stumble. She was able to flash one quick look to her rear and was horrified to see Melwas after her. It had never entered her head he would have a horse so near and he was riding like a madman to catch up. She was under no illusions about what would happen if she allowed him to succeed. Wild plans shot through her mind. She dared not ride at this pace in what was still gloom and it would be fatal to lead this madman to where Ygraine and Hoel would be waiting.

Finally, gritting her teeth, she knew she had no alternative. She collected her mount together, and eased the pace back into a more controlled canter so letting him catch up. This was going to be one of the biggest gambles of her life.

Melwas was just behind her now. 'I'll have you, you bitch!' he shouted, drawing alongside on her right. Bracha acted fast. She pulled back savagely on the reins and her horse protestingly juddered to a slithering halt. Melwas shot past, carried by his own momentum. As he did so, Bracha withdrew her dagger, made sure she gripped it tightly and stabbed at the man just behind his left arm. The knife sank in sweetly, sliding between two ribs, puncturing the lung, then Bracha's horse halted and stood breathing heavily.

The mount of Melwas went on a very few paces, then automatically slowed as the man slipped from its back and crashed down on the earth, driving the knife in so deep only the hilt now showed.

Bracha vaulted from her horse and ran back. Melwas lay still half on one side now, and he gasped as a pink frothy blood began to cascade from his mouth. Bracha stared down at him, waiting to feel something, anything. This was the first man she had ever killed. The first human life she had ever taken yet she felt nothing but tremendous relief that she was free and relatively safe. Who would have thought it possible that Melwas, of all people, knew the difference between a healing plant and a common weed.

His eyes were open, filled with hatred, as she looked down at him, then they closed as he died. Once she was certain of this, Bracha bent forward, and with a certain amount of force, withdrew her dagger. She wiped it clean on the grass, put it back in its sheath then, snatching hold of the reins to save her horse from bolting, she was heartily sick.

With an incredible effort of will she struggled on to her horse's back again as the other loose horse took it into its head, as horses always will, to go back to that which was familiar and join companions. Bracha pulled a face and winced. She knew she would soon go into shock, but she must get away from this immediate area. It would take very little time for a search party to come out, her tracks would still be too fresh and easy to read.

She rode purely by automatic instinct and headed towards the agreed meeting spot. Both Ygraine and Hoel came to meet her with a glad cry of greeting, instantly frozen at the damage to her face. Although he had been warned by her mother, Hoel was appalled. Ygraine, shocked into silence by everything she'd been told in the last few hours, could not stifle a gasp of horror. Then her mind reverted automatically. Hoel no longer needed a healer. But here was a nice fresh patient!

Bracha knew her only too well and stifled a groan of anticipation. 'Forget it, certainly right now! I have just killed Melwas. It won't take long for him to be discovered and his horse has bolted back to the tun. I have escaped and defied my father. There'll be a search party out after us very quickly. We should get away from this area as fast as we can and hide our tracks as best as possible. Let's ride!'

* * *

Ralf awoke with all the din from much shouting and bellowing. Only one man could make such an uproar at what was an ungodly time. He went to move quickly, then halted and winced at the drums in his head. For once his guts were quiet but he knew this would not last when food began to work its way through.

He dressed laboriously as his wife appeared. Her eyes were cold, and he winced at their expression as guilt plunged a knife into his conscience.

'I am sorry,' he said and meant it. 'I know, I went mad, but—' and he paused, unable to put in words what the pain was like when it struck. 'I'll go and see her, apologise and make my peace.'

'Don't bother!' Elesa told him tartly. 'She's gone!'

Ralf was stunned at this. 'But I never gave her permission—' he began with irritation rising once more.

Elesa felt for him, but kept her features quite impassive. 'You are nothing but a stupid man! As if you could stop real love with orders! If we had had Bracha's sense, when we were her age, we would have had longer together. And don't you start to bristle at me! If you lift one finger in my direction I'll—I'll—divorce you!' and her jaws clicked together.

'You wouldn't?' Ralf blurted with deep shock, all his gut's pains completely obliterated.

'No? Try me!' Elesa grated even though, her heart was breaking.

'Where's she gone? Do you know?'

Elesa made herself appear very stern. 'Yes I do and you'll be the last person to learn!'

Ralf knew when he was beaten and sat half-sulking like a small boy whose mock spear had been taken away from him and broken.

'I'll send someone to ride after her with a peace offering,' he began, when Gandar rushed in unceremoniously. 'The horse of Melwas came back without him, and a couple of the scouts went out looking and they found Melwas. Very dead. One horse was going away from his body at a good hard gallop. They recognise the hoof prints. It was one of ours!'

Ralf and Elesa exchanged rapid looks. Gandar explained what he knew from the returning scouts.

'Knifed in the lung. Then he fell off, drove the knife in further and died. A very neat job!' Gandar finished approvingly, for he was just one who had been at the receiving end of the tun's greatest bully.

Elesa nodded to herself, then looked deep into her husband's eyes. 'You trained her well, Ralf. *Now* do you believe how serious she is about the Saxon?'

TWELVE

Hoel hesitated. So far, everything had gone incredibly well. The three of them had ridden off to the Romano traders and the deal had been struck about the horses. They all had three good mounts now, and although the lady Bracha had received some very queer looks from the traders at the state of her face, they had been too polite to ask any pointed questions. Perhaps also the fact that she wore a golden torque around her neck had been more than enough to stifle their curiosity. Certainly run-of-the-mill Britons could never own such fine and expensive jewellery.

The trouble was, Hoel had to admit, that the torque could also be a double-edged sword. Not only did it indicate high rank and breeding but it was something impossible to forget. He went back over the lady Elesa's words and thought he understood everything that had taken place leading to this particular moment.

The lady Bracha had also left a sealed communication with detailed instructions that it was to be given to one person only. She had also given a description, and finally they had parted company. The Lady and Ygraine had ridden off in one specific direction, and he knew they intended to take great pains to hide their passage from any tracker. It crossed his mind to wonder how good they would be at this?

That was out of his hands though. He had his own duty to do and was suddenly uncertain, and not confident about his capability. He had never envisaged he would ever be in such a situation, but the thought that he was now a freeman was the straw to which he clutched when his confidence quivered.

One enormous problem had hit him right from the start, but he had kept this to himself. Now that he was alone, riding solo, it kept recurring. He only had one horse! Yet there would be two of them. He had even considered bartering for an extra horse but riding one and leading one would require considerable explanation for inquisitive Saxons. It would be obvious that the extra horse would be connected with another person.

With great reluctance, he had not taken an extra horse so now he mulled over the ways and means of extracting a man from a camp with only one horse between them. It would be the height of stupidity to steal from the Saxons and have a whole army chasing after him.

He was a deeply worried young man. The whole of his life depended solely upon what took place during the next handful of days. The very thought of failing and being hurled back into slavery was too appalling to contemplate. He simply had to succeed, and he had no idea how to go about this.

He knew he was approaching the Saxon encampment long before he saw activity. There was a pall of smoke ahead from many cooking fires. There were interesting odours of roast meat, which made his mouth water. He was young, and seemed perpetually hungry. He dismounted and carefully took his horse into a small stand of trees, where there were many low shrubs. He tethered the animal in such a manner that it could graze on the grass growing in between the shrubs yet still be unable to bolt.

There was another point causing him enormous worry. His very precious manumission document had been written in the Britons' normal runic script. Would the Saxons be able to read this? His confidence teetered again as he sneaked silently, then slithered on his belly up a slight slope. Very gently, he peeped over, and below lay the Saxon encampment. He studied it carefully, and wondered where on earth, among all these warriors, and even womenfolk, he would be able to find one specific person.

He lay a long time, taking it all in. Horses here, some cattle there, tents in another place, slaves at the rear and everywhere warriors sharpening weapons, reinforcing shields, practising strokes with one another, other little groups chatting together drinking what he guessed was ale.

It was not a noisy place and his belly rumbled. He made a snap decision, stood and plodded down the hill to where he had already seen a watchful sentry. Just turning away from talking to the man was another Saxon, whose eyes narrowed at his approach.

'You! Who are you? What are you doing here? I haven't seen you before?' Cutha challenged, while the sentry half lowered his spear warningly.

Hoel took a deep breath and prepared to lie in his teeth. 'I am only passing through and smelt the roast meat, and I am hungry,' he said by way of what he hoped was a reasonable reply. 'I come from over there,' and he nodded vaguely in a direction which could have been anywhere.

'Passing through to where?' Cutha demanded to know suspiciously.

'I have no family. They are all dead from sickness or disease in the last year so I thought I would explore and see a bit of life before looking for a girl and settling down.'

'You are a runaway slave!' Cutha accused hotly.

Hoel had sense enough not to overdo the lying. 'It's true, I was a slave but I was able to do a favour for a lady and she gave me my freedom. Here, read this!' and now it was his turn to challenge.

Cutha took the document and read it very

carefully. He was not all that familiar with the runic script, but he knew someone who was. 'Come with me!' he ordered brusquely.

With thumping heart Hoel obeyed. Cutha eyed him surreptitiously, as they walked along together.

'What did you do to get this?' he wanted to know.

Hoel was ahead of him now. 'It was for a lady. Surely it would be wrong of me to say?'

Cutha turned that over in his mind. A suspicion had arisen. Something did not quite gel here, yet, he had no idea what it was. The young man seemed harmless enough. He did not carry a sword or shield. He had a frank open face and he seemed so incredibly young and innocent. But was he?

He stopped by the animal pens and Hoel stared in amazement and shock. He could only just recognise the young Saxon who had so attracted the Lady Bracha. The young man was in the filthiest of clothing, and was obviously preparing to be harnessed up with the most enormous load. Both of his eyes were black-ringed, and his face was swollen and must have been very tender.

Hoel was lost for words. It flashed through his mind that as his lady had received a beating her young man certainly had too.

'Cenberht, read this for me!' and Cutha shoved the document before the two black eyes.

Cenberht stood frozen a second as he recognised the young slave from *her* tun, then a wave of wild hope flashed through him. He bent his head, and swiftly read the runic writing.

'Well? Cutha demanded.

Cenberht took a deep breath and made himself concentrate. 'It's a manumission document stating that this bearer is a free man!' and he flashed a look at Hoel. If only he could speak to him privately. What was going on? Why was he here? He looked at the document again and saw that it had been signed by his lover's mother. His heart now throbbed with unexpected hope, and he wished his uncle was 1,000 miles away.

Cutha grunted to himself still very uneasy, without quite knowing why. He looked at Hoel and Cenberht in turn, and chewed his bottom lip thoughtfully. Something stank but what?

'Very well,' he said finally. 'I'll see you get something to eat,' he told Hoel. While turning something over, Cutha could be swift and exceedingly bright when he decided not to play the fool. It had not taken him any time at all to figure out from where this new freedom man had come, nor why.

He turned and looked over into the distance. He had not approved of his brother's actions, which had been far too brutal. What was so terrible about young love, even if they came from opposing sides? He was torn between loyalty to his brother king and his natural empathy for a young couple who were obviously prepared to defy the world just to be together. Was this such a terrible crime really?

He turned back. 'You, boy, go over there and get something to eat, then come back here. Cenberht, I think sometimes you might just be the biggest fool in creation, but never let it be said that Uncle Cutha stood in your way. Don't go out labouring today.'

'The king?' Cenberht asked anxiously.

Cutha considered. 'He is going to be very engaged in a war council meeting at which I will attend with others. I think also, it will never enter his head that anyone has the gall to defy him! Stay here, talk to this young man, decide what has to be done and I do not want to know a word. Is that clear? I can go so far, but no further!' he said, and his words had a little ring of kindness.

Cenberht gulped. 'But what about you, Uncle? When the king finds out—!' and his sentence tailed off unhappily.

Cutha gave him a hearty slap on the shoulders. 'Don't you worry about me, nephew! I've been putting up with and standing up to my big brother for more years that you know exist!' he said in a lighter tone, then his voice became serious again. 'But make sure you plan properly, act carefully, and don't get yourself caught in any compromising situation. I can only protect you so far. Is that

187

clear?'

Cenberht's heart swelled with gratitude and hope. He knew he would be forever indebted to an uncle whom he had never properly appreciated before. He ducked his head politely, and threw the older man a winning smile. Then Cutha turned on his heel and strolled away to the king's war band meeting. Thank all the gods this was taking place right here and now. He wondered what would happen, would Cenberht make it to his beloved? It was a loaded question, because one thing was certain, if the king caught him again, he would be lucky not to be executed in one of Ceawlin's rages.

Hoel came back to the animal pens. His belly felt better for a hot stew and he looked around uneasily. Where was that bossy, older Saxon? Then he caught Cenberht's eyes, large and filled with worry and anxiety. Throwing another look around to ensure they were alone he entered the pen.

'I know you!' Cenberht said in a low voice. 'Have you come from—?'

'The lady Elesa sent me as well as the lady Bracha,' Hoel said, then began a rapid explanation.

Cenberht listened and winced as he heard about his beloved's thrashing. As Hoel finished and again threw a quick look in all directions, Cenberht's head sank with despair. Beaten by her father and all for him. Misery filled him, then he lifted his head, his expression grim.

'I've been sent to help you get away and to take you to the lady Bracha,' Hoel finished softly. 'Are you watched?'

Cenberht pulled a face. 'During the day, yes. I'm being used as a pack animal. The king ordered it after he had beaten me!'

Hoel blinked. This explanation he had never expected . . .What kind of a man was this king who behaved like this to one of his warriors? His bewilderment showed.

Cenberht understood. Now was certainly the time for more explanations. He was realistic enough to know further elaboration was required. With this young man's help he might have an outside chance of escape. He itched to know if there was some positive plan.

'The king is my father!'

Hoel was staggered with shock. 'What!'

'Base-born though,' Cenberht told him and gave a brief résumé of his life to date. 'For years I was a nonentity in the king's eyes until he wanted something done that no one else could do because they lacked my flair for languages!' he said ironically. 'I expect you now know that Calthus was implanted as a king's spy?'

Hoel certainly did not know and his eyes opened wide with this revelation. 'So that was why he ran with you!' he marvelled. 'I thought he was just taking a chance to bolt for freedom!'

It had never entered Elesa's head to give her opinion of Calthus. Time had been of the essence up against Ralf's temper. She was not particularly interested either as her whole being had been concentrated upon her daughter and what an ex-slave could do to help her.

'I never guessed!' Hoel said, shaking his head. 'I just thought he was doing a runner— like me!'

'It was my father's plan from start to finish and kept highly secret!' Cenberht explained dryly. 'Even I knew nothing until the last breathless gasp! Calthus is now a highly respected noble!'

Now Hoel was speechless with sheer admiration for a king who could plan so astutely and yet risk his own flesh and blood on such a dangerous enterprise without hesitation, whether base born or not.

Cenberht felt ready to explode with frustration now. 'What are your plans?'

Hoel recollected his wits scattered by shock after shock. 'For us to bolt together at night but there is one great problem right now. I only have one horse,' and he explained the reason. 'It would have been far too dangerous for me to ride in here leading a spare. As it is, I bumped into that older, grumpy Saxon who was suspicious from the start. Will he be dangerous, do you think?'

'Uncle Cutha? Oh no, he will do what he can to help but he has to be careful because of his position here!' Cenberht explained.

Hoel let out a gasp as these words registered. 'Uncle? That means—he is the king's brother!' His head revolved with complicated permutations and it crossed his mind to wonder if the lady Bracha and her lovely mother knew, then commonsense told him they could not. Such valuable information would have been trumpeted far and wide especially against Chief Ralf.

'Well!' was all he could get out for a moment, then he flogged his wits back into action again. 'Your lady's mother gave pelts to barter with the Romanos so we stopped there. Changed our horses and your lady made arrangements for two good fresh horses to be available for us if we can but get there riding double.'

'Then?'

'There will also be a note for you detailing how to ride to where your lady and a companion have hidden themselves!' Hoel explained soberly. Could the two of them do it? It was all an enormous gamble from start to finish.

A man hove into view, whistling tunelessly as a warning and Cutha halted before both of them. He studied each of them in turn. Cenberht had fresh, wild hope in his eyes while Hoel eyed him with apprehension.

'The council meeting has closed for the time being and it won't be long before it is dusk because I think we're going to have some rain. The sentries hate getting themselves wet. They can be like a lot of old women. I expect most of them will try and find themselves a good place of shelter. All the hounds are just as bad. They'll be undercover, if they can find somewhere,' he said with a very heavy hint.

Cutha gave an exaggerated look up at the sky, then turned and stared fixedly at his nephew.

'Thank you, Uncle. I owe you!'

Cutha gave a snort. 'You owe me nothing if someone sees you, especially if that someone happens to be my big brother!'

Then Cutha turned on his heels and walked away in a casual manner, though his mind raced at speed. Quite suddenly, he knew he wanted the boy to succeed. There was certainly much more to Cenberht than ever met the eye.

Hoel watched him go and turned back to his companion. 'Lord, we should slip away as soon as we can. Once the rain starts!'

Cenberht gave him a warm and sincere smile. 'Don't call me Lord. I'm just the same as you, no better no worse!'

'Weapons?' Hoel wanted to know anxiously.

Cenberht thought for a few seconds, then shook his head. 'Just our eating daggers. Nothing else for the moment. Two of us on a horse are going to be enough for the animal. Once we can get to the traders perhaps we'll find enough goods were left to pay for a spear and shield each?'

Hoel had no idea. The bartering had all been done by the lady Bracha. Cenberht looked around and their little part of the encampment was empty. He eyed the sky carefully, and the dark clouds were scurrying in their direction. Nightfall would be rapid. Then suddenly, as he watched, it began to rain. First a light shower, then the precipitation increased. He flashed a look at Hoel and nodded.

The two of them slid from the animal pen and ran into the gloom, heading for some trees. Hoel kept his wits about him and began to veer to one side to where he had left the horse. The rain now teemed down in a steady curtain and it had a bite of chill in it. With Hoel in the lead, pausing now and again to peer ahead and scan for any possible sentry taking shelter and half hidden, they ran up the slope.

Hoel let out a huge sigh of relief as they found the very bored horse had eaten everything within reach and seemed almost pleased to regard them with pricked ears and half-lifted head. Swiftly Hoel untied the animal and vaulted onto his back. Cenberht quickly followed suit, and moving only at a very careful walk, they began to leave the

Saxon encampment behind.

The rain now sheeted down and it had begun to get very cold indeed. Cenberht hazarded a guess it was winter's last fling. Already, some of the rain droplets held little flakes of sleet, and he counted his blessings. They could not have prayed to all the spirits for better weather in which to make a run.

*   *   *

'Gone? Gone! What do you mean—gone?' Ceawlin growled, then swore lustily.

Cutha eyed him coolly and felt enormous relief. Cenberht and his companion had been given the luck of all those spirits in which to do their runner. Today, all traces of the heavy rain had vanished. The sky was blue overhead and the sun beamed down. So far so good, he told himself, and felt smugly pleased with his personal part in this exercise.

Now came the storm, but he was not in the slightest bit perturbed. He faced his brother, most amused at the expression of outrage on Ceawlin's face.

'I won't have it!' Ceawlin bawled. 'Someone helped him. They had to. The sentries were lax!'

'We did happen to have some very heavy rain last evening!' Cutha reminded him ironically.

'I'll have those sentries executed!' Ceawlin

continued almost unabated.

Cutha felt his own anger rise, a rare emotion for him. 'You will do nothing of the kind unless you want a definite guarantee of losing against the Britons at Deorham!'

That halted Ceawlin in his emotional tracks. 'What is that supposed to mean?' he hurled at his brother, then was suddenly a little puzzled. This was not the usual Cutha who considered life one enormous joke. Cutha, the greedy, the womaniser, the prankster. The man who faced him, although he had known him all his life, had changed. His brother faced him squarely, stern-faced, stone-cold sober without a joke in mind. 'Explain yourself!' he barked imperiously.

Now it was Cutha's turn to scowl. 'All right, but don't you use that bombastic tone with me either. I am your brother, remember? Think back to when we were boys. Oh yes, you often beat me in fights, because you were older and bigger, but how much good did it do you? I used to walk away and leave you. It never took long for you to come running after me either. Without me you were very lonely!' he snapped.

Ceawlin was astounded. 'I am the king!'

Cutha let out a snort of disparagement. 'So what!' he shouted back. 'A king is no good without men behind him. Now just you sit down and listen to me for once!'

Ceawlin was so taken aback he did as he was told and plonked down on a stool. Cutha actually bristled! He could not last remember when his brother squared up to him because he certainly meant something now. His whole stance and body language were one of total belligerence. Even his fists were balled in to clubs. Ceawlin suspected he could still best his brother in a brawl yet he hesitated. 'Well, spit it out then!' he grated. He was livid with himself, his brother, Cenberht, and the whole world in general.

'Everyone here knows you have had a flaming row with the son who did your dirty work for you at considerable risk to his life. They do not understand what is happening, and the men do not like it either. Cenberht's stock has shot up high in their eyes, and that incidentally, includes Crida and Calthus,' and he paused to make sure his words were going home. 'And you expect them to fight a battle against a dangerous enemy when you put on such a display of childish anger? Grow up a bit! Stop trying to be so regal! Kings rule by consent, remember! Do you want the men to drift away and give their allegiance elsewhere? They can, you know!'

Ceawlin knew this perfectly well yet he was more deeply shocked than he cared to show. 'But—!' he began in his defence.

'There are no buts!' Cutha roared at him. 'You have made an absolute fool of yourself over Cenberht, and you know it. Be man enough to admit it—to me at least!' he challenged.

Ceawlin scowled and muttered something coarse. 'Oh all right—but someone had to have helped him. I've a right to know who this traitor is!'

Cutha burst out laughing at the petulant look on his brother's face. 'If you want it straight and can control yourself, I did! So pick the bones out of that!' Cutha retorted, then stood, arms crossed, waiting with interest. He realised he had no fear of his larger brother now. Had he ever had any really, he asked himself? Muscles were not everything.

'You!' Ceawlin gasped. 'But how could you? You know how he has humiliated me with that noble and the girl's father!'

'Hah!' Cutha spat. 'Now we come down to the nitty-gritty of it all! It's your pride that's hurt! You don't really give a toss about my nephew! Yes that's right. He is my flesh and blood also, and, like you, I've been tardy acknowledging the fact—but not too late, I hope?' and his voice dropped to a softer tone. 'Think back, brother! Remember the boy's mother? Remember how much you loved her and how angry you were when our father took you away to fight when she was pregnant. Think back to how bitter you were when you returned and discovered she had died in childbirth!'

Ceawlin did and lowered his head. They had been very black days, and the most bitter part of them was his personal castigation. He could have married before leaving to fight. He could have stood up to his father. Why hadn't he? Because he had lacked the guts.

'I remember,' he whispered miserably. Then flashed a look at Cutha. 'You arranged it all?'

'No, he had a helper come to do that!' and Cutha then went into a detailed explanation. 'It's quite likely, the girl took hell from her father, because we are not exactly flavour of the month with the Britons. I've asked around and have a pretty rounded picture of her. She too is not the type to back down. She is tough. She has backbone and it's made of steel. I think you will find she will be a very worthy mate for your son. And there is another point, you would do well to consider!'

'What's that?' Ceawlin grumbled, getting rather fed up with his brother's diatribe.

Cutha dragged up another stool and sat to face his brother. Deep down he admired him, he liked him and respected him, yet he had never felt as close as they were right now. 'When we beat the Britons do you want trouble afterwards with them? A race who has been thrashed bears tremendous resentment . . . it runs bitter, deep and is long-lasting. The Romans had to learn that the hard way. Profit by their experience. Encourage this match, and by so doing, you will unite two peoples. It will make your life much easier if you do not have to keep looking over your shoulder to see whether a spear is coming in your direction.'

Ceawlin was stunned with amazement. 'I didn't think you had all this in you!' he grumbled.

Cutha laughed, leaned forward and slapped him on one shoulder. 'Did you bother to try and find out before?' he riposted.

'How the hell could I when you spend so much time womanising?' Ceawlin growled, then grinned.

He felt better already. Secretly he was filled with admiration and pride for Cenberht, whose actions put his own when young to shame.

THIRTEEN

Bracha felt dreadful. She had not felt like that to start with. There had been the swift bartering with the traders, then Hoel had ridden off. She and Ygraine had taken great pains to hide their tracks as best as possible over streams and hard ground.

They had camped this first night in a small clump of trees and eaten cold food. Both of them were silent, each immersed in complicated thoughts. Bracha was astounded to find she was homesick, and she did not like this one bit. How was it possible for her to want to be in the tun, with her father, when somewhere out there was her beloved?

What if Hoel was unable to make contact with him? This thought nagged at her constantly until she felt almost sick with stress. She could not envisage any life without Cenberht at her side, because her feelings she knew were as strong as ever.

She lay awake, wrapped in animal skins, unable to sleep, and suddenly she started to wish she had something positive in which to believe. Were there still evil spirits, which only came out at night? If so, did they really do battle with the good ones? Or did Christ watch over all who believed? What about the old beliefs, those of the long-vanished Druids?

For centuries Druidism had been the religion of her ancestors, and, even today, in these modern times it had often crossed her mind that perhaps some of the old people preferred to follow ancient proven beliefs. Mona in particular. If she had lived a few hundred years ago Mona would certainly have followed these ways in which time was marked by counting nights and not days.

The Saxons were, she knew, absolute pagans so where did Cenberht stand in such matters? In what did his family believe—if he had any? It had finally occurred to her that with their chances to talk freely having been so limited, never once had either of them referred to breeding, kith or kin. Perhaps he was an orphan? Like Ygraine and Gandar.

Their parents had died very young, one in battle and the other through disease. They had been mutually reared by the tribe. Did the Saxons do the same? What were the Saxons really like? She was not so naive as to consider they all took after her beloved.

These thoughts multiplied and enlarged as her imagination produced worry after fresh worry. There was only Ygraine to talk to now, and she seemed to have lost her tongue completely. It never entered her head that her companion's mind was also horribly confused and upset.

Ygraine had been appalled at her friend's beating and the reason, as Elesa had taken great pains to explain everything. When she had learned Hoel had been freed to perform a specific commission she had been so thrilled. Now, though, upon sober reflection, she was riddled with worry. As a free man he could go where and when he liked, without let or hindrance. He could make eyes at any free female in the land, who was of equal rank. So where did this leave her? She was honest enough to acknowledge that at no time had Hoel ever expressed a preference for her. It was true he was grateful for her healing ministrations, but Ygraine wanted more than that. She wanted him as her man, her mate. Her heart ached to know what he really thought about her.

She felt utterly miserable, consumed with a

thousand doubts and had no idea what to do next. She had eyed Bracha a few times, willing her to talk, but her friend was completely lost in her own misery. Even the knowledge that Mona now looked upon her with favour seemed almost of no consequence.

They both spent an utterly wretched night and mounted their horses with the dawn. Each looked at the other and pulled a face, then Bracha nodded her head.

'We should reach our destination point today. If we can find a little sheltered dell we could try a small fire and have something hot. We have been lucky with the weather so far, but I wonder—?'

'What is happening?' Ygraine finished for her. 'It's the not knowing, that is the worst!' and she bit her lip unhappily.

It hit Bracha that Ygraine had her own worries and doubts, and it was easy to see in which way they headed. She managed a rueful grin: 'We are not a very happy couple right now. All this upset caused by men, but I suppose they are worth it! Now let's ride.'

They rode in silence at a gentle trot, both of them highly alert to everything around. The land seemed to be empty, even the wild animals were scarce but both of them knew this was an illusion. Somewhere around, hidden among the trees and forests, would be wolves, boars, bears and deer.

They were well armed with a sword, spear,

small shield and eating dagger, which could double up to make a lethal weapon as Melwas had found to his cost. Bracha had pushed this killing from her mind and deposited it in the realms of history. It had been her or him plus her drive and purpose, aided by the speed of her youth, which had given her the victory.

Ygraine and Hoel had been shocked and astounded when told the whole incident then they had eyed each other reflectively. Bracha had done something that now put her in the bracket of blooded warrior. She did not realise what enormous respect she had acquired so suddenly and unexpectedly. To talk of killing someone was one thing but to actually do it was a huge matter. She was indeed the daughter of a chief in their joint eyes, but did her Cenberht equal her? Only time would tell, they both knew, and Hoel had ridden off on his commission aware that he was dealing with someone a cut above the ordinary.

Ygraine was aware that she regarded her companion in a very different light to that in which she had held her when they lived in the tun. She knew now that she looked up to Bracha in a manner that had been inconceivable before.

'There!' Bracha said suddenly and pointed. 'That has to be the place. Down on our left is Deorham. That piece of flat land on top of that lower hill is where the battle will take place.'

'We will have a good view from here, as this hill is higher,' Ygraine said and paused. 'Will you go down to join in the fight?'

This was a question Bracha had constantly asked herself. 'How could I with Cenberht? We would have to fight on opposing sides. I simply could not bear it,' she said slowly.

Ygraine understood. Then her eyes narrowed. 'I don't think we are going to be alone. I am sure I saw movement beyond those bushes, to the right of the trees!'

Bracha stared hard and automatically checked her weapons, while Ygraine copied. They had both been very well trained, and now went on to the alert. They pulled their horses back to a very controlled walk, then Bracha took the lead as befitted her status. Suddenly she pulled her horse back to a halt and gasped with shock, and Ygraine copied as they dismounted.

'How on earth did you get here before us?' Bracha wanted to know.

Mona gave them a smile, while her eyes twinkled. 'Some of us can get around very fast indeed without horses!'

The healer beckoned them forward behind the shrubs to where a small shelter had been erected. It was nothing more really than a roof of saplings tied down. whose opened sides were made from shrubs that had been broken off at ground level and plunged into the earth. It was a crude but effective shelter against all but the most inclement weather. There was a very small fire burning made from very dry wood which gave virtually no smoke. Over this spits had been fashioned and two rabbits were slowly turning. To one side was a container of fresh water, and on the other Mona had laid fur skins for her bed.

Both of the girls looked at it, and each other and smiled mutually. It was the most comfortable, cosy camp imaginable, and they doubted they could have done as well.

Mona smiled at their amazement. How naive the young could be thinking only their generation could manage matters.

'Welcome to my camp, girls. I intend to stay here until after the battle, when my services will of course be needed. You are welcome to stay with me and your menfolk too, when they return.'

Bracha looked deep into the wise eyes. 'They will come?' she asked, her voice filled with anxiety.

'Yes please tell, Mona!' Ygraine begged.

Mona reverted to her usual, enigmatic conversation. 'They will come if this is willed!'

*   *   *

Ceawlin did not hurry. He was far too wise and battle-experienced to make such an error. He wanted his men completely fresh and willing for the fight to come. It was also a matter of practicalities. To move many men and all their equipment could turn into a logistical nightmare, unless handled very competently.

Only a few selected women were allowed to come as followers and their task would be to attend to the wounded after the healers had dealt with them. He liked to feed his men well so carefully chosen cattle brought up the rearguard escorting by trusted slaves. Animals would be slaughtered as and when required. There was plenty of water from streams and springs, because the king knew alcohol was imprudent before hard fighting.

They came in a reasonably straight line, with scouts out at the front and on the flanks. Cutha found himself in his usual roving position, riding here and there, checking on everything possible and picking out what information he could, as and when.

One evening he sat with his brother, gnawing roast beef, while around twinkled many fires as the men copied. These night camps held on the war path were good occasions, because of the men's general camaraderie. They were all in excellent humour, itching to go to war and to receive their share of any suitable plunder.

'I rode out to the Romano traders this morning,' he told Ceawlin who did not reply immediately, because he was savouring a particularly tender piece of beef.

'And?'

'Cenberht and that young freed slave made it there all right, riding double bank on a horse near the verge of foundering. They took two fresh horses, some basic weapons and rode off again not pausing for anything.'

'Is that so?' Ceawlin drawled. 'So what could he steal to barter?' he asked a little wearily.

'Nothing! It had all been arranged in advance by the female, who, incidentally, had been given a hell of a beating!' Cutha told him.

Ceawlin sat up straight, instantly alert, as his mind revolved in a number of interesting directions. So the girl too had been thrashed, yet had been to the traders and arranged all this? This was an interesting and unforeseen development. He knew he was now getting exceedingly curious about the female, who certainly appeared to have more about her than the usual run-of-the-mill. Was it this that Cenberht had seen? It made a very interesting question.

Cutha read him easily. 'Both of the traders were very interested in the fact that boy and girl had been beaten when they came from opposite races!'

Ceawlin grunted . . . 'What did you tell them?'

'Nothing, because it was none of their damned business!' Cutha replied somewhat tartly.

'Did they say any of the Britons had been

around?'

Cutha nodded. 'As a matter of fact they did. They were looking for the girl. It appears they had a huge bully of a man called Melwas, and it seems when the girl bolted he tried to stop her. Because of what happened they were after her for that as well!'

'So?' Ceawlin asked. He was getting interested. 'What did the girl do to him?'

'Oh! Only killed him!' Cutha drawled.

'What!'

'That's right and I remember now Calthus talking about a swine of a Briton. Huge man as well and a very good fighter. Cenberht's lover simply killed him because he was in her way!'

Ceawlin was shocked into total silence. He could not imagine any Saxon female doing this, and he eyed his brother thoughtfully. 'I wonder just what my son—and me—might be taking on! This is getting very interesting indeed. I bet the pair of them have bolted to some pre-arranged hiding place and won't show their faces until it's all over. Well! Well! Killed a big warrior indeed!' he marvelled, half to himself. Then a smug look appeared on his face.

'Stop gloating!' Cutha rebuked. 'Remember what you did to your son?'

Ceawlin winced. 'But I didn't know!' and he knew it was a pathetic excuse. He had the grace to blush and break eye contact first as Cutha smirked.

Cutha knew when to let the matter drop. 'By tomorrow, we will be within easy striking distance of Bath. What are your plans there?'

Ceawlin shook his head. 'We can always come back and sack Bath. Our priority now is to thrash the Britons at this place of theirs, which they call Deorham.'

Cutha frowned a little. 'Your plans?'

Ceawlin threw him a wolfish look and quietly explained in detail. 'It's worked before. Why not again?'

Cutha strolled a few paces, turning it all over in his mind. 'We will be outnumbered. Those three local kings will be able to muster a vast number of warriors. We could be outnumbered at least three to one,' and he paused to reflect. 'We need luck with the weather for your plan to succeed!'

'I think we'll get it too!' Ceawlin said confidently. 'Now here is what I want you to do in person. I want the men divided in three groups, each to have a leader who can keep absolute control at all times. I want the men to stand back and not move one toe until I give the command and then they will only advance as I have explained.'

Cutha nodded. This made sense given his brother's plan. 'Ideally we could do with the discipline of the old Roman legions,' he added thoughtfully, then threw his brother a lopsided grin. 'But that's too much to hope for as we are Saxons.'

These had always been Ceawlin's thoughts, because it was the old Romans' rigid military discipline that had given them so many victories against the ancient Britons. The only way in which these people's ancestors had been able to score points was in their superb guerrilla tactics. These latter would be totally useless in the set piece battle, which now loomed.

'Calthus would make an excellent leader for one of the groups, because he is so highly respected after the service he's done for us. Crida could lead the other, because he spent those handful of days living with these people. Knowing him, he would not miss much either,' Ceawlin said thoughtfully.

'And the third group?'

Ceawlin gave a low laugh, and a deep chuckle. 'We will have that pleasure!'

*　　　*　　　*

Mona was the oldest of the three of them, yet her instincts were more highly attuned than those of either Bracha or Ygraine. The sun had already started angling down to the west when the healer stepped forward and looked around keenly.

'What is it?' Bracha asked anxiously, suddenly highly alert. Had a group from her home tun found them at last, and she was to be taken back to defend herself for the death

210

of Melwas? Her face set in a grim line. Not if she could help it. Not now, that would be just too cruel for words.

Ygraine read her mind, and loosened her sword and stepped forward to stand by her friend's side. She gave her a look of encouragement and Bracha's heart throbbed with warmth and gratitude. It was quite incredible how recent circumstances had managed to change a loose-mouthed, silly-headed girl into this serious and obviously very reliable companion.

Mona turned her head from side to side, picking up vibes only available to her very acute and uncanny senses.

'Two horses coming, and very slowly,' she told the girls. 'The horses are exhausted and not far short of foundering because they have been ridden long, hard and fast!'

Bracha and Ygraine looked at her with respectful admiration. How did she know all this when they were so much younger and completely mystified?

'There!' and Mona pointed down and to one side.

Bracha and Ygraine swivelled to where she pointed and very slowly two men came into view, riding horses whose heads hung low from total exhaustion. Both girls recognised their men, and instinctively ran forward with enthusiastic greetings.

Bracha halted as Cenberht wearily

211

dismounted, turned to her and opened his arms in greeting. She flung herself at him, and revelled in his hug while he kissed her again and again. Then she pushed herself back and looked with horror at his bruised and battered face.

'You too?' she asked sadly. 'Which Saxon did this?' she questioned with rising anger, ready to take on the whole Saxon nation. Cenberht's two black eyes had now turned a dingy yellow. How dare someone do this to her lover over her? Her maternal possessiveness was purely instinctive.

Cenberht eyed her face in return. Even though her swellings were receding nothing could hide the fact she too had received a thrashing. And she—a girl! What vicious lout had done this? And Cenberht felt his own rage rise high.

'Who?' he grated and ran his fingers gently over her face.

'My father!' she admitted heavily.

'Because of me and the fact I'm Saxon?'

Bracha gave him a rueful nod. 'But who beat you? Why did your king allow it?'

Now it was Cenberht's turn and his lips grimaced. 'It was because you are a Briton and my father too did it. He is—the king!'

Bracha was thunderstruck. Bereft of all speech. Ygraine, Hoel and Mona had overheard and they stood in an odd frozen tableau of astonishment. Only Hoel had known. Mona turned her eyes upon him, and smiled enigmatically then gave a tiny nod of approval. Cenberht flashed her a grateful look, then turned back to his sweetheart.

'We had little enough time as it was,' Cenberht explained to Bracha, 'and it means nothing at all really, because you see—I am base-born! I believe the king had intended to marry my mother once she was pregnant with me but he went off to war, and that was it. By the time he returned I had arrived upon the scene and my poor mother was dead. I was brought up, rather loosely by the rest of my people!' and now it was his turn to wait anxiously. What did the Britons as a race think of one so placed? He was ignorant about their culture as Bracha was concerning general Saxon ethics.

Bracha had started to recover from her shock and let out a disparaging snort: 'You had no say in the matter, and I take you as you are and for better and worse too!' she intoned, very serious now.

Ygraine beamed at her friend and Mona nodded approvingly. Hoel stood a little flat-footed, rather out of this complicated conversation. He did not quite know what to do with himself. He was proud his mission had been accomplished so satisfactorily, then Ygraine turned and gave him a spontaneous hug of pride.

'I think you've been marvellous!' she

praised and meant every word with sincerity.

Hoel looked deeply into her eyes. This girl had given him back his health after rescuing him. He owed her a lot, yet in the tun there had been something about her character that had irritated him enormously. Now he regarded her thoughtfully. This was not the same girl at all. She had changed beyond recognition. She had suddenly grown up, acquired astonishing maturity and was another person entirely. He felt a flare of deep interest, took her arm possessively and walked her to one side.

'You have really changed. And I like this new you!' he told her sincerely. 'How do you feel about considering me as a suitor? I have nothing to give you to plight a troth. Not yet at least. If you would be prepared to wait—?' he asked, and waited anxiously.

Ygraine felt herself blush. Sudden bashfulness overwhelmed her as she nodded. 'I don't need tokens. They are only material objects,' she said with sudden wisdom. 'Your word is good enough for me!'

Mona had missed nothing. She was perfectly well aware a very bad time was yet to come, and it would be soon. She beckoned the two couples to her, put Ygraine's hand in that of Hoel's and Bracha's in Cenberht's. Then, closing her eyes, she muttered a few words in a tongue that not one of the four of them had ever heard before. Finally, she opened her eyes and a beaming smile lit her face, making her seem years younger.

'I have blessed both of you couples in the olden way,' she said in a soft but firm voice. 'In my eyes and in the eyes of my Druidic ancestors you are joined one to the other from this moment onwards. If later on, you wish to regularise these unions, then so be it! I have spoken!' she told them and turned back to her little shelter.

FOURTEEN

Ceawlin stared around, taking his time to note every detail. He had taken great pains not to hurry the men as they skirted Bath and there was method in his madness. It was not just that he wanted them fresh to fight, he wanted them to be impatient and itching to battle as much from boredom as anything else. Now they had made their night camp less than half a mile from where the Britons waited. He had prudently arranged a tight line of sentries, knowing the British glee at bursting forth unexpectedly to create mayhem with their natural guerrilla tactics of old.

Cutha stood with him. 'Do you think they will try it on tonight?'

Ceawlin shrugged. 'If they do they'll get a shock. I doubt a mouse could slip through unobserved and the men can spring to arms in seconds. Personally, I think they want a set piece battle. They are so confident with their superior numbers it is going to prove their undoing!' and he grinned in anticipation of victory.

Cutha considered thoughtfully. He had blind faith in his brother's tactical ability but there was a huge horde of men ready to face them. He could tell that from the noise they made. The Saxon war band was almost silent in comparison. Just the usual murmur of men chatting together after they had eaten preparatory to settling down for a good night's sleep but with weapons to hand for instant action.

The dawn came, and the sun rose early, but the two brothers were earlier still. Ceawlin studied the sky carefully, noted the already cloudless sky, tested to make sure there was only the slightest breeze and nodded in satisfaction.

'It's going to work!' he told Cutha, who had been conducting his own examination of the sky and who agreed. 'About when?'

Ceawlin debated for a few seconds only. His men would stand only so much hanging around inactive when there was a highly vociferous enemy so near.

'My instinct will tell me that. Just make sure our men are kept under rigid control. The first one who steps out of line will answer to my sword. Make sure that goes to every man and that Calthus and Crida also understand!'

Just then, a very young sentry trotted up. 'Sire! Over on that hill. There are people!' he blurted out.

Ceawlin and Cutha swung round instantly. What did this mean? Reserves being held back for a counter-attack and some impatient men had shown themselves? This could be serious.

The brothers screwed up their eyes and could make out five figures. 'Now who can they be?' Cutha wanted to know.

'You!' Ceawlin barked. 'You are younger and will have sharper eyes. What details can you give me?'

The sentry was delighted to oblige a king for whom he had the utmost respect and admiration. It took him only a few seconds' study.

'Two males and three females. One of the females is much older than the other two. And the males are young like me,' he said.

'Well I'll be—' Ceawlin started, then nodded to the sentry to dismiss him.

'Do you think—?' Cutha asked hesitantly.

Ceawlin's eyes glowed with admiration. 'I don't think—I know!' he exclaimed. 'That is my wayward, bloody-minded, pigheaded, obstinate son and one of the females with him will be the Briton who is a warrior killer. Who would have thought it!' he murmured, and gave a tiny shake to his head. 'Him and that freed slave made it here after all, and met up with that girl and her companion, who has obviously prearranged the whole thing. I shall very much look forward to meeting that female,' he added dryly. 'She has made a fool of me!'

Cutha was speechless for a moment then he had to grin. 'In that case, you may have to watch out. She might pick you as her next target!'

Ceawlin gnawed his lip thoughtfully, then looked soberly at Cutha. 'Aren't you forgetting something?' and he became very serious now. 'They have picked that place to watch the battle. How is the girl going to react when I decimate her people?' and he paused reflectively. 'When she does come down she is to be watched. There is no telling what she will do, and Cenberht, being with her, after everything, will be on her side. Not mine!'

Cutha nodded at these cold facts. It was true, no matter how well a battle was planned nearly always something arose which was totally unexpected. Neither of them had made plans for such a personal equation. He felt unease fill him. 'But the other female?'

Ceawlin again considered then nodded slowly. 'I bet she is a healer and her services are going to be very much required before nightfall.'

*　　*　　*

As the sun advanced the watchers on the adjacent hill realised they were so placed that they did indeed have a bird's eye view with such an excellent visibility. Their stomachs were full, their horses were neatly tethered, and they sat down on the short tufted grass to watch.

Both Cenberht and Bracha had very mixed and opposite feelings and Mona, sitting tactfully to one side away from the two couples, was able to study them in profile and read their emotions so simply.

Ygraine and Hoel sat together holding hands, each highly pleased with the other after their consummation when they had taken themselves away from the shelter. Cenberht and Bracha had moved off in the opposite direction and now they sat with his arm around her shoulders.

Mona was perfectly well aware of the joining which had taken place under the night sky and it had her full approval. Perhaps even now, both girls had started the long journey towards motherhood and the foundation of what would be a new race. It was something she had never experienced and there were times when she felt great sadness at having missed out on one of life's great wonders.

She would then remind herself that perhaps she had been put on earth not to reproduce naturally but to use her natural skills for the benefit of all, friend or foe. Her duty now would be to pass on her vast range of knowledge and experience to Ygraine, who would one day travel tribes in her place. With a man at her side she would cope easily with children and the whole of the land would benefit. Once this had happened, Mona knew she would be quite content to find a quiet, hidden spot and lay down a burden that sometimes became hugely onerous.

First though, they all had to get through what Mona knew was going to be a traumatic day, especially for Bracha. She allowed herself to reminisce about Ralf and Elesa. Deep down, with her usual vivid honesty, she had to admit that Elesa had always been the better mate for wonderful Ralf. Where she had been concerned, it had never been meant to happen.

Bracha studied the battlefield below in great detail. There had been ample time for the Britons to erect obstacles and defences. Two ramparts had been hastily constructed to halt any wild dash of the Saxons, and behind these the Britons waited eagerly. She thought she could see her father, moving with three other men to whom everyone deferred: the three Kings, Condidan, Farinmail and Coinmail.

She felt her heart swell with pride and kept looking ahead. Poor Cenberht, what a dreadful day this was going to turn out to be for him. She looked sideways and studied the Saxons who seemed pitifully few in numbers. Walking slowly, almost ponderously, was a very big man and she knew, with unerring instinct, this was King Ceawlin, Cenberht's odious father.

By now, the Britons were wildly excited, ready for instant battle, hurling vocal challenges at the invaders. They pranced around, ready for action, waving their weapons, showing what splendid fighters they were going to be. Many of the challenges they hurled at the Saxons were earthy and ribald and as some of the words floated up to Bracha's ears she went a bit pink.

She was astonished to see the Saxons still held back by the king and wondered what on earth was the matter with him. He had come to invade and fight. As he continued to hold his position it entered her mind that perhaps the huge gathering the three kings had mustered was now too daunting for him. Serve him right, she said to herself, then sneaked a glance at her lover's face.

It was impassive. She could read nothing. She turned her attention back to her own people who continued to bellow challenges and wave their weapons invitingly. And still the Saxons were held back by the dominant power of their king.

The sun continued its climb in the sky, and now the watchers on the hill began to feel uncomfortable, but there was no proper shade for them. Mona understood in full, and pity filled her. So much blood was going to be spilled and although no military tactician herself it had not taken long for Mona to work out the Saxon king's tactics. They were clever, and they would be terminal. Was it a good or a bad thing that Bracha did not yet understand?

She looked over at the young Saxon who had an unreadable mask on his face. He sat as if frozen and Mona sensed he had already worked out Ceawlin's ploy. He said nothing, because there was nothing he could say, and Mona gritted her jaws together tightly. When would Bracha understand? What would she then do? She could only pray her love for the young Saxon would halt her from rushing down to join in the battle once the consequences were understood.

By now, it was really warm, and the watchers had started to sweat. Cenberht studied the Britons very carefully. It was true, they were still prancing around, roaring challenges and waving their weapons but he fancied some of them were not quite as exuberant.

A battle sword could be a heavy object to wield at the best of times, let alone to be lethal in a fight. A shield was no lightweight affair either, and those Britons below had been racing around, prancing and bellowing their challenges for a long time now. They had wasted valuable energy, which should have been kept back for the actual battle. They had poured with sweat from their own exertions, and it was certain there would not be enough water on top of that hill to replenish every man.

Cenberht turned his attention to his father. All the time the king had been walking backwards and forwards, prudently keeping just out of range, tormenting the Britons. One or two had even jumped over their defensive barriers but the king's personal gesith, his bodyguard, had leaped into action, bustled their king out of the way, and engaged the rash Britons.

This had taken place three times and, each time the king had been pushed to safety, the Britons had howled their mockery even more. Cenberht understood the tactics well now. He dare not turn and look at his beloved because he knew he would give his thoughts away.

Why couldn't she understand exactly what was taking place before her very eyes?

Cenberht looked up at the sky. The sun was almost a searing ball of heat, where they sat. At the slightly lower altitude of the battlefield, the heat would be scorching. Those British warriors must be almost sweated dry. Even if there were slaves enough to bring up water from the bottom where nestled the actual village, there would only be enough to make each man crave for more.

Then the scenario began to change before the watchers' eyes. Ceawlin exchanged a look with Cutha and Cenberht saw him throw a barely perceptible nod. In his turn Cutha lifted first his right, then his left hand to the flanks with a prearranged gesture. Cutha withdrew his own sword at last, stepped up to his brother's side as the king turned and roared, 'Now!'

* * *

Bracha gave a gasp as the Saxons stormed forward in a wave of battle enthusiasm. They crested the first line of defence, crushing the waiting Britons without stopping then they hurled forward in an uncheckable wave of vicious killing.

She was aghast and turned to Cenberht, felt the warmth of his hand and also saw the look of pity in his eyes. Quite suddenly, something large and heavy sank to the pit of her stomach. A natural warning screamed through her mind as she struggled to understand.

Then it hit her. 'Oh no!' she gasped. 'Our men have exhausted themselves before the fight has even begun, and it must be so hot down there, with so little water. I see it all now. Your king—your father—has been baiting them all the time, while his army has stood quietly reserving its strength! No! He's not going to—!'

'Don't look, Bracha!' Cenberht cried as the slaughter continued. The Britons were valiantly brave but their efforts were almost completely puny. Man met man. Woman met man. The spears had all been thrown and now it was the case of swords and battle axes. The barbaric clashing of metals often sent sparks splashing out. Those men who favoured a battleaxe were busy decapitating heads, while a comrade defended with a sword, the men working in well practised teams.

The Britons retaliated furiously but now they were exhausted prematurely, and they began to fall back, still fighting, but pushed relentlessly rearward by the Saxon horde, retreating foot by foot, blade against blade but they had no chance at all. They were totally exhausted and dehydrated. Men panted, struggling to force air into labouring lungs, legs had turned to quivering jelly, it was an effort now to clash sword blade against sword blade. Legs trembled and the Britons began to reel in their tracks.

Back, then back even more with the Britons driven until they were at the edge of the hill. A gallant number endeavoured to hold the Saxons in this bloody hand-to-hand fighting, but to no avail. Right on the front line, leading and encouraging his men, Ceawlin was a killing machine, with his gesith and brother to hand.

Then Ceawlin halted, stepped back one pace to eye the debacle before him while he made a very swift calculation, and he knew the time had come. The Britons ahead were on the verge of breaking into a fast retreat downhill. He turned, lifted his sword vertically and waved it to the right and then the left.

Immediately Calthus and Crida reacted. Each leader spun around and bellowed at his men, then with another quite unstoppable tide of very fresh and eager warriors, the flanks burst into a roar as they raced forward to right and left.

The Britons had broken completely and were streaming down the hill intent on reaching their horses and safety. The flanks charged forward in hot pursuit to right and left while Ceawlin concentrated on the main fighting, which was diminishing before his eyes. It was a bloodbath.

The escaping Britons tumbled and slithered down the hill, utterly exhausted, and nearly crazy for water. The flanking warriors followed them and, as Ceawlin had learned from past experience, they curved inwards at the base of the hill. Saxon met Saxon, in a completed circle and the Britons, now at the end of their fighting tether, were shocked and totally demoralised to come up against a unexpected wall of flashing weapons from fresh men. They were hopelessly trapped in a vicious nutcracker action from which the only escape was death.

Bracha understood. Tears streamed down her face unchecked, unashamed and bitter at her people's defeat. She began to sob, great cries breaking from her lips. 'We have lost!' she wailed and Cenberht grabbed her to his chest while his own heart swelled with pain as he shared her grief.

It had all been inevitable from the start. Cenberht realised now the depth of his father's intellect and natural cunning, going right back to the time when he had persuaded a fine Saxon warrior to infiltrate the enemy's position as a lowly slave. His admiration for his father reached a pinnacle and he knew for the rest of his life he would look upon King Ceawlin with very new eyes.

His heart filled with pity for his beloved Bracha, now a member of a discredited and defeated race about to be enslaved to the power of the Saxons. 'Over my dead body!' he told himself coldly. 'Bracha is mine. No man, no king will hurt one hair of her head.' He was armed. He was but one man, but without hesitation he knew he would defy his father, the king, if it meant dying himself.

Ygraine and Hoel were stunned into total silence with horror. They had not quite known what to expect. Neither of them had ever been a party to war and this almost simple slaughter affected them terribly. Ygraine felt the tears streaming down her cheeks, quite out of control as a silent Hoel could only hold her in his arms.

Mona was unaffected. Her instincts had

been ahead of all of them. That deep secret vein inside her, which often predicted the future in an uncanny manner, had pre-warned her of the inevitability of it all from the very start. She looked at the two couples, studied them for a few seconds, then her gaze rested on Bracha who, very slowly, stood up.

Mona walked over and rested both hands on Bracha's shoulders and looked deep into her eyes, seeing misery and appalled horror.

'You knew?' Bracha said, and her voice croaked.

Mona gave her a sad smile and a gentle nod. 'I did not say, because I would not have been believed and anyhow words cannot halt the inevitable. It is the march of time and progress, which you will neither understand nor believe at this moment. Cenberht, she really needs you now!' she said with a heavy meaning. 'I must go!'

'Go where?' Ygraine managed to blurt out.

Mona gave her a long look and pointed down below 'To where I am very much needed. They and others like me around. They will have known, like me. You have not seen them, because we keep ourselves hidden until our skills are needed. There will be fighters down there who will be glad to greet the poppy flower drink.'

Ygraine gave a gulp, then moved to the healer's side with Hoel a pace behind. 'I am coming with you,' Ygraine said bravely, quite aware she was now going to see horrific sights. 'I am your pupil! My duty is with you!' and firmness now came into her voice.

Mona smiled with approval. A battlefield was not the most ideal place in which to start to train an acolyte but her pupil's reactions in the next hour or so would show her mental fibre. The healer looked into the younger eyes which held hers firmly and noted the upright stance and new determination. Hoel stepped forward by Ygraine's side in such a positive gesture of solidarity that Mona now knew, for the rest of the life granted to her, she would have two faithful followers.

Bracha turned to Cenberht, her eyes filled with abject misery, and she took a deep breath. She willed her tears to cease with a burst of rigid mental control. She held her head with pride. She was a member of a defeated race, but her spirit was unbowed and unbroken.

Gritting her teeth, Bracha took the first step down the hill to face the inevitable horror. The other four followed, allowing her the supreme privilege of leadership.

They took their time, picking their steps carefully so their descent was dignified. Ceawlin nudged his brother and pointed. He had wiped the blood from his sword on the edge of his trousers and placed it back in its sheath.

'Oh! Oh! Trouble coming?' Cutha murmured to him.

'We'll soon find out!' Ceawlin replied dryly.

Around him, his men were busy. Bodies were being laid out in a rough and ready line. Those who still lived had been helped to another area. The walking wounded went elsewhere, while the prisoners who had a chance of living were guarded in a separate area. The latter were pitifully few in number. Both of the brothers knew that at the bottom of the hill there would only be bodies because the fighting there would have been of the most ferocious nature.

Britons trying to escape would have been up against wildly excited and very fresh Saxons who would have resented being held in reserve. They would have gone out of their way to make up for this so it was unlikely any quarter would be asked for, let alone given.

The brothers studied the group as they neared and now Mona took the lead. Her eyes went everywhere, estimating and assessing, already working out where she should start. She totally ignored the king and his brother as being of no consequence whatsoever.

Ceawlin knew his duty and stepped before her. He looked down at her and bowed his head with the deepest respect, and his brother copied.

'You are, sad to say, welcome,' Ceawlin told Mona. She turned dark, unfathomable eyes upon him for just a fleeting second, then dismissed him with an almost imperious gesture.

Ygraine and Hoel hovered at her side respectfully.

'You and you!' Ceawlin bawled at two of his men. 'Here!' he rasped. 'Follow the healer and obey her instantly at the peril of your own lives!' he barked, then bowed his head once more and stepped aside. Mona walked forward, eyes riveted on the nearest wounded, leading her little procession like a queen.

Cenberht stepped forward, shielding Bracha. He faced the king, very much on edge, one hand resting meaningfully on his sword hilt, which gesture Ceawlin did not miss. He recognised his son's strong body language. It shrieked silently for him to hear. *This female is mine. Touch her at your peril!*

Ceawlin's eyebrows shot up, but he did not make the insulting mistake of grinning. He turned curious and very serious eyes on the girl. Bracha faced him four-square. She held her head with pride and looked unflinchingly into his eyes. There was nothing subservient in her proud stance. They looked at each other, words unnecessary.

Cenberht felt as if he were balanced on a sword edge. He looked from one to the other and frowned. Still not a word was spoken from either of them and Cenberht gulped with nerves. If one of them would only say something, even if it was but to swear at the other.

231

Then Bracha knew what had to be done. This was the victor. The King. She was a well-bred chief's daughter, albeit on the losing side. She stepped back half a pace, then slowly, but oh so proudly, bowed her head to the winner. She lifted it again, and held eye contact once more, her stare steady, challenging and defiant. Her people were beaten. She was not.

Ceawlin had the crazy idea that if he issued a personal challenge, here and now, she would take him up on it. He stood, feet slightly apart, but firmly planted and stared hard back. She was no beauty, that was for sure, yet she would strip well. Her shoulders were broad for a girl, which meant she had always exercised. She had nice big breasts, which he had always admired as he had always been a breast man himself. Her waist was slim above very wide hips.

Good childbearing material, he thought to himself and totalled up all these points. She stood with her feet apart, her body braced against whatever life would throw at her. She was taller than most Saxon girls yet there did not seem to be anything ultra-extraordinary about her.

But there must be for Cenberht to act so possessively as he still was right now. He frowned a little and looked into her eyes again, and it hit him with tremendous force. It was her personality, her spirit and an obvious high intelligence; all these combined into some ethereal aura which flowed from her to him as he continued to stand and look. For a few seconds he had the ridiculous feeling she was mesmerising him with sheer mental power. It was he who broke eye contact first.

He flashed a weird look at his son. Was it possible Cenberht would be able to control the power that was wrapped up in this one girl? He blinked. 'Well,' he added to himself. 'That's his chosen problem not mine!'

He turned back to Bracha. 'Do you wish to look for anyone?' he asked gently. 'Though it won't be pretty!' he warned meaningfully.

Bracha nodded firmly. Her jaw lifted a fraction and her lips screwed tight. 'My father,' she told him.

Ceawlin nodded sagely. He too would like to meet the man who had sired such a girl. 'Come, girl. I think they call you Bracha. I'll address you that way, if I may?'

You cunning old devil, Cenberht told himself because Bracha fell right away. Her antagonism vanished as the king held out a hand of support so she could step over a dead Saxon. 'Come, my dear. I will escort you in person!'

Cenberht pulled a face, then shook his head with admiration as his father turned on his full Saxon charm. Cutha had been nearby watching the byplay, and he moved his head near to that of his nephew. 'The king can still run rings around you when charm is needed!' he quipped. 'I can see your Bracha is just about ready to eat from his hand!'

It was horrendous. A fight with naked metal weapons leaves nothing to the imagination and Bracha was aghast. She had never seen so many dead people at once, and arms, legs and heads were around, giving proof of the destructive power of sword and battle axe.

There were many wounded lying everywhere, many with quite horrific injuries and over all was the noise, the cries and groans of agonised distress, the pleas for help, the calls for aid to stifle dreadful pain.

Bracha flashed a look around and saw Mona bending over a man with Ygraine and Hoel in close attendance plus the two selected guards. Dotted around other healing women had mysteriously appeared and she gulped uneasily. She watched Mona study one warrior, who was still alive, but in agony. Mona flashed a look at one of the men escorting her and gave an imperceptible nod. Immediately, he stepped forward, and in one flashing action drove his sword point into the man's heart, and put him out of his misery.

Mona continued scanning both the living and the dead, then she beckoned Ygraine and pointed. It was Gandar who must have died instantly from the wound of a half-severed neck. Then it was Bracha's turn to come across Ricole's body. She felt sudden tears in her eyes. There had never been any love between them but she was a tribal member and she had died bravely in battle.

Bracha felt a terrible lump in her throat. She should have been by her side, she was the daughter of the chief, and Ricole's death showed her up. Guilt filled her. She had been concerned only with herself while her old enemy had faced the foe gallantly.

She spoke to Cenberht. 'We could not stand each other. Yet here she is dead, while I'm alive. It's all wrong somehow and—' Her voice broke with guilt and shame.

Cenberht was swift to understand her dilemma. 'I too should have been down here, standing shoulder to shoulder with my father. He did not shirk fighting, even though the king. He shared with his men, and both of us will have to outlive this day and these sights,' he told her with sudden wisdom. 'Perhaps it was preordained for some reason we do not yet understand!'

Ceawlin paused to look at where three bodies lay together, but apart from the rest. He pointed and waived his right hand. 'The three kings,' he explained. 'They died with their men and were men of men themselves!' he praised in tribute.

It was Bracha who spotted him first and she let out a cry. 'Father!'

Ceawlin and Cenberht hurried over as Bracha dropped to her knees. She looked down at Ralf's hideous wound. His abdomen had been slashed open, and his intestines sprawled half from the belly onto the sodden earth

'Mona!' Bracha shrieked. Then she looked up at the king and his son. Her eyes brimmed with tears. The beating and the past were forgotten. She grabbed Cenberht's hand and pulled him forward so that Ralf could see.

'My Saxon,' she explained and Ralf turned his dying eyes and gazed upwards in deep study. 'His name is Cenberht and he is the king's son!'

Ralf's eyes opened wide with astonishment, then Ceawlin displayed himself. The king dropped down to his knees. 'Yes, this is my son. A born troublemaker as I suspect is your daughter. When they have their own, they will understand, won't they?'

'I simply had no idea!' Ralf murmured. 'Young people today are hot-headed, bloody-minded, dumb at the wrong times, think they know it all and sometimes are not worth bothering with!'

Ceawlin threw him a slow smile. 'My sentiments exactly. Don't worry, I'll keep an eye on them and if necessary, straighten them out when it becomes needed!' he promised seriously.

'Bracha, look after your mother. She knew this would be the end as did Mona,' and Ralf struggled with his final words. 'You see, I have been dying for quite a long time. Something

236

growing inside me. Mona has known and your mother slowly guessed. I'd rather go out this way. It's a man's way. It is a warrior's way!'

Then Mona was by his side, tilting a small beaker that held cloudy liquid. She bent over her first love, placed the beaker to his lips and encouraged him to drink.

'Come, Ralf,' she said in a kind voice. 'This is the honourable way to go now. You will drift off into sleep and go and join our ancestors!'

Mona turned and looked up at the king, then pointedly nodded at the young couple. She flashed him a silent message, which he was astute enough to understand immediately.

He lifted Bracha with one arm and nudged Cenberht. He gave him a hard look. 'Take her back to her tun and her mother. Stay with her. Later on, perhaps tomorrow I will ride down to join you. Now get her away from here!' he lowered his voice and hissed.

Cenberht approved as did Mona who let Ralf's head slump back with death. The healer stood and watched as Cenberht escorted her slowly away. They would climb back up the hill to collect their horses and ride to Bracha's home, where it had all started only a short while ago.

The king and the healer watched their backs grow smaller, as they started up the hill. Then they looked at each other.

'Those two are your future, King Ceawlin. Upon them you can build a new race of Briton and Saxon combined. You have great power, King. Use it wisely and our united peoples will thrive to make a new race entirely. Love, especially young love, is the most powerful emotion ever. It cannot be stopped or baulked. So don't waste any more effort on trying to halt it. Those two will give you fine children!'

Ceawlin nodded thoughtfully as the young couple breasted the top of the hill, mounted up and rode out of his sight. It was indeed his new beginning.

Historical Note

The historians consider that the Battle of Deorham was of very great significance towards the founding of the English race. It took place about 577 AD.

The Britons had by and large, been Christians. The Saxons were pagans, so Christianity vanished, not to emerge again until it was re-introduced by St Augustine in the next century.

History does not say much more about King Ceawlin, though records show that in 584 AD he and his brother Cutha fought at a place called Fethan Leag, where Cutha was killed. Then Ceawlin went on to take many towns and 'receive greater spoils of war'. He died in either 591 or 593 AD. He was succeeded by Coel from Cutha's line, who then reigned for seven years.

There is no absolute proof that Cenberht was Ceawlin's son though it is thought likely. For the sake of the story I have bastardised him. A king by the name of Caedwalla ruled between 685 and 688 who descended from Cenberht's line. It is from Ceawlin's personal line we are given the great King Ine.

Horses, as we know them today, i.e. above fifteen hands, were unknown in Britain then. The native stock were pretty tough ponies but for simplicity's sake I have used the word 'horse' loosely instead of 'pony'.